Praise for
Christmas at Mistletoe Lake

"*Christmas at Mistletoe Lake* was a labor of love not just in the conception of Robin's story, but also in the making of the film. An inspiring filmic journey for all involved where passion, vision, and commitment yielded a whole far greater than the sum of the parts." ~ Robert Vaughn, Executive Producer

"Reilly Shore was such a joy to bring to life. Robin created a beautifully strong, independent and driven woman who happens to love Christmas as much as I do. She's fun and a little quirky with a heart that's unmatched. I love how open and honest she is and how far she is willing to go for those she cares about. I hope you'll love Reilly has much as I did." ~ Genelle Williams, Actress

Christmas on Mistletoe Lake

ROBIN SEAMUS DUNNE

Vinspire Publishing, LLC
www.VinspirePublishing.com

For Everly

Author's Note

All my life, from childhood to the present, lake country has held a special place in my heart. Growing up in the city, I would jump at any chance to join friends or family on a trip to their cottage.

In recent years, we've spent many Christmases at the lake, and there's no other place I'd rather be during the holidays. When the opportunity arose to write and direct a Christmas movie, my first inspiration was for the story to take place in this setting.

Bringing *Christmas on Mistletoe Lake* to the screen was something of a marathon, not an uncommon experience in the film and television business, made even more challenging by the obstacles that were presented by the global events of 2020/2021.

As laborious and patience-testing as it was, one happy accident of the situation was that I was presented with the chance to try my hand at novelizing the film. Writing the novel not only gave me the experience of getting to know these characters and the story on an even more intimate level, but it also allowed me to expand and explore this world that is very much a part of me.

Having had zero previous experience in the medium, as you might imagine, delving into the world of novel-writing was intimidating and at times overwhelming. However, as I got further into the process, I found that there was a tremendous freedom in the transformation of the story into a novel.

Film and television are mediums of brevity and expedience. Books are refreshingly free of time constraints. Both invite their audiences on a journey—film being visual, a novel being experiential.

With our year-long delay in the shooting schedule, I was able to complete an early first draft of the book before the cameras began rolling. Having the manuscript on set proved to be a tremendous asset to not only myself, but to our lead actors, as well.

It is quite special for me now having seen both the novel and movie come to life from start to finish.

Prologue

Reilly Shore lay awake in bed, listening to the winter wind outside her bedroom dusting the window with granular snow. It was a comforting sound, as though the house were one of those snow cones her parents would buy for her and her sister on their family excursions to the mall.

She didn't particularly like the snow cones, with their artificially bright colors that left her tongue tie dyed for hours afterward. Come to think of it, she didn't actually like the malls. There were so many they had visited in the different places they had lived. All different but the same.

Ubiquitous music echoing off the overly polished floors, a smorgasbord of conflicting smells wafting from the food court, and a double layer cake of retail shops selling sunglasses, cell phones, and sneakers, bookended by two department stores that sold all the same stuff and more. Still, going to the mall on a weekend afternoon was something normal suburban people did, and that gave Reilly a comforting feeling.

The wheezing sound of the wind outside also served the dual purpose of drowning out the droning metronome of her sister's dead-to-the-world snores below her. It seemed an eternity that Reilly had been lying sleeplessly on the top bunk of her bed. She kept her eyes closed tightly, somehow trying to trick herself into *thinking* she was asleep, but it was of no use.

Deciding to check the time once more, Reilly turned and looked at the digital clock radio which sat atop the six-disk CD changer boombox the girls had gotten for Christmas last year. The glowing neon red numbers on the clock stared back at her indifferently. *4:17 am.*

Reilly sighed with silent impatience. What seemed like forever had only been nine minutes. This night was interminable. Then again, she was used to it. She'd always experienced a wonderfully agonizing excitement every Christmas Eve since she could remember. However, this year it was different. A whole new level of ebullient energy swirled in her stomach.

It was precisely because of this type of exhilarated insomnia that Reilly's parents instituted the *Christmas Eve Rule*: no family member was allowed out of bed—and, more importantly, was forbidden to wake any other family member—on Christmas morning until dawn, at the earliest.

This family rule hadn't been instituted because of her sister, Tara. No way. If Rip Van Winkle gave her a title shot, Tara would certainly come away victorious as the world's sound-sleeping champ. Reilly could never understand how anyone would be able to diffuse their excitement enough to sleep so restfully on a night like Christmas Eve.

It wasn't the thought of Christmas presents that set the roller coaster of stomach butterflies in motion for her, though those were certainly a lovely perk. It was more than that. It represented a time when she and her family could be free of all the noise of the outside world, simply being content with each other's company and feeling *at home.*

The cherry-red neon digit furthest to the right on the clock switched from a seven to an eight. It was now *4:18 am.* She turned and stared at the dark bedroom ceiling three feet above her.

The darkened face of Eddie Vedder and his bandmates stared back at her. Reilly wasn't a huge fan of the band, nor was she guilty of putting posters on the bedroom ceiling. That was all Tara's doing. But, since they were sharing a bedroom, and Tara reluctantly acquiesced at Reilly decorating the room with Christmas ornaments starting bright and early on November 1st, she couldn't very well take issue with Tara's rock posters. As close as the two sisters were, their esthetic tastes could not be more opposite.

Reilly blinked in the darkness, giving a momentary break in her vision, as though looking through a View-Master stuck on the same slide. There was no way she was going to be mentally or physically able to stay in bed until...*dawn?* This house that they'd moved into only eight months before was further north than the last place they lived. That meant the winter sun wouldn't start to peek over the horizon until after seven. *That's three hours from now,* she thought with an excitement bordering on panic. There was no way she could lay awake in bed for that long.

Like a cat burglar—which, for the first few years of her life she thought referred to a criminal who went around stealing people's pets—Reilly noiselessly climbed down the blonde lacquered ladder of her IKEA bunk bed. As her foot pressed on the thick, brand-new bedroom rug, Reilly walked toward the bedroom door, carefully making sure to time her steps in sync with her sister's snores.

When Reilly arrived at the top landing, she peered through the darkness at her parents' bedroom door. As her eyes adjusted to the opaque, windowless hallway, she saw that the door was slightly ajar. This is where the game got real.

Like her sister, Reilly's mother Carole was a sound sleeper who needed three or four cups of strong morning coffee before fully shaking off the depths of her nightly slumbers. Reilly's father Bruce was the complete opposite. They could never have any clocks that ticked, taps that dripped, or neighborhood dogs that barked within a three-mile radius of wherever they lived.

As she silently creeped out onto the brand-new hardwood floor, Reilly felt the fresh varnish under her foot. The smoothness of the floor's surface gave it a freshly Zambonied hockey rink feel. In her mind's ear, Reilly heard the countless conversations surrounding the floor between her mother and father.

"Why would anyone cover up such beautiful mahogany *with carpet*?" Her mom could never seem to keep the mild disdain from creeping into her voice when they talked about the past decorating mistakes of their various houses' previous owners. This was often followed by the requisite discussion and calculations of how their work would increase the value of said houses, which—given that their business was house-flipping—was a good thing. The term house-flipping was yet another momentarily misleading term for Reilly's young mind. She quickly learned, however, that it was in no way similar to what one did with pancakes or coins.

Reilly carefully made sure to take a large step over the floor vent next to the bathroom, remembering that it tended to creak like a sedated frog. As she padded down the stairs two at a time on the balls of her feet, she was greeted by the glowing Christmas tree, with its lights metronomically switching from blue-to-green-to-red standing in the living room's bay window.

The recently purchased tree—amazingly the family's first one—was adorned with heaps of tinsel, and the plastic branches were weighed down heavily with what now seemed like an overly enthusiastic number of ornaments.

When they had made the decision—when *Reilly* had made the decision, to be precise—to stay home for Christmas instead of going away like they always did, the family went a little overboard making sure to get every accessory possible for their newest holiday purchase. Everything imaginable was hanging on that tree—except for popcorn garland, which got eaten before it could be strung together and spiraled through the branches.

The living room still smelled like the fire Reilly and Tara had begged to have as a Christmas Eve treat before they went to bed. Their family stockings were pinned up on the mantle above. There were also the lingering perfumes of last night's dinner, the sisters' attempt at a lasagna that resulted in mixed reviews, which wrestled with the aftertaste scent of new carpet.

Slowly and quietly, Reilly plugged in the lights, then sat in the oversized armchair and watched as the tree bathed her in flashing, festive glows.

Blue. Red. Green. Blue. Red. Green.

She didn't think to sneak a peek through the loose seams of the wrapping paper on the gifts tucked under the tree. She was confident about what she and Tara were getting—a Nintendo and a couple of Pound Puppies—both all the rage at the moment. No, Reilly simply wanted to sit and let this feeling soak into her heart like a tea bag into a cup of warm water.

Finally, this felt like a true Christmas at a real home. She had never remembered being at home for Christmas before in her life. Never like being here at 9 Deanewood Crescent.

As she happily stared out at the deserted street outside, the freshly fallen snow yet to be trampled on by foot or tire, she pictured how many more Christmases the family would have here. She hoped they would be countless.

Reilly often had this silly daydream…she knew it was silly, wouldn't dream of telling anyone, yet she still allowed herself to privately live in the fanciful imagination…about never moving from this neighborhood. Even when she became an adult, she could buy the house next door, her parents could help her fix it up, and her sister Tara could buy the one on the opposite side.

Reilly might even marry Tommy McNeil, the paper boy who lived across the street. Tara could marry Tommy's younger brother Keith, whom she protested to be disgusted by, though Reilly had suspicions otherwise. They could all live there forever, happily having summer barbecues in green grassy backyards, autumn walks through the rainbow trees in the ravine just beyond, and visiting for coffee and cake on rainy spring days. And Christmases. Always Christmases.

A gust of wind-chilled breeze caused the For Sale sign spiked into the front lawn to metallically rattle, pulling Reilly from her reverie. The week-old sign only represented mild anxiety for her, as did the photographed face imprinted on it.

Corin Pumphrey, her parents' real estate agent. Always with that toothy smile—the very same one he used for the photo on his signs and his business cards. Reilly had an unspoken suspicion that those teeth weren't Mr. Pumphrey's own. Well, of course, they were his, in the sense that they didn't belong to anyone else.

However, Reilly believed that he'd purchased them and had a dentist screw them into his mouth as opposed to the ones that grew out of his gums naturally. They had the vague look of the white tiles her parents were so fond of installing in their remodeled bathrooms. Reilly figured this was why Mr. Pumphrey was so happy to show them off.

Between that and his perpetually ruddy complexion with accompanying sheen of perspiration, as though he were in the habit of spraying himself generously with Pam before ringing the doorbell, he looked like a Saturday-morning cartoon character. But Reilly couldn't help but feel sorry for Mr. Pumphrey. No matter how much he smiled, his eyes always looked sad. She imagined he ate most of his meals alone.

He always said the very same thing every time he'd seen Reilly or Tara, "There they are! The jet-set sisters!" For some reason, this annoyed Tara, which she made embarrassingly obvious by not smiling whenever he said it. The source of her annoyance was probably due to the fact that even though the family DID move quite a bit—once a year on average—it never involved the setting of any jets. And it wasn't in the least bit glamorous.

The moist, rotund real estate agent also annoyed Tara because he smelled like a case of empty beer bottles and Speed Stick. Reilly didn't particularly like these qualities, either, but it was less about the man himself, than what he *represented* that disturbed her. Every time Mr. Pumphrey started coming around, she knew they'd inevitably be moving soon. It was usually just when they'd finally gotten comfortable somewhere. Moving always meant enrolling in new schools, trying to make new friends, and adjusting to a new life.

However, this time felt different. This house. This *home*. With its crooked picket fence along the skinny driveway to the tiny garage in the back with the leaky roof. That crabapple tree in the front yard, with its splayed-out octopus branches that begged to be climbed. Her parents' mantra was *Always buy the worst house on the best street.*

While this house couldn't be described as *the worst,* Reilly felt that the family had finally hit their stride here. This Christmas would seal the deal. There was no way her parents would ever want to part with this place. There was no reason why they couldn't still flip other houses, just as long as they didn't flip this one. No matter how good an offer they'd get. No matter if the legendary bidding war that the real estate agent promised actually happened. No matter if-

Suddenly, something outside caught Reilly's eye, which caused the locomotive of her thoughts to come to a sparky, screeching halt.

There was no way. It must be the sleep in her eyes playing tricks on her. Or the condensation on the glass causing an optical illusion. She stood, frozen, statue-like in the living room as the cycle of Christmas tree lights each took turns in shifting primary colors.

Blue. Red. Green. Blue. Red. Green.

With her rising anxiety and disbelief each rushing to gain the upper hand over her, two jockeys of emotion racing to be the first over the finish line, Reilly forced herself to move toward the window and climb up on the sill. With the sleeve of her pajama top, she brushed away the fog on the inside of the glass and peered out. Sure enough, there it was. Desperate, she rubbed her eyes, picking out the pebbly sleep in the corners—as though that might make a difference. She looked again. It was still there.

A sticker. Slightly crooked and pasted onto the real estate sign, blocking out some of the wording beneath. The sticker was newer and shinier than the rest of the grungy cardboard. Large red letters against a white backdrop, like the inverse of a stop sign, but commanding equal attention, that read...

SOLD.

That sticker couldn't have been there very long. A day? Surely if it had been there any longer, she would have seen it before now. There must be a mistake. It was the in-between hours of Christmas Eve and Christmas Day. Who would be thinking of buying a house at this time of year? As Reilly racked her wheeling brain to try to put the puzzle pieces together, a dank feeling of dread rose in her heart, like a slow but steady plumbing leak in a basement.

She felt the choking ball of sadness rising in her throat as her vision pulsed with anxiety through her eyeballs. All the while the clock-like lights from the Christmas Tree flashed aloofly.

Blue. Red. Green. Blue. Red. Green.

A torrent of unhappy thoughts poured through Reilly's head. This meant they'd most certainly be moving in a month or two. When did this actually happen? And when did her parents plan on telling them?

Reilly sat back down into the armchair, as though her legs were slowly melting out of despair. Thankfully the shabby-chic chair was there to catch her. So, this was it. This was goodbye to 9 Deanewood Crescent. As the spinning butterflies in her stomach shriveled into dust, Reilly couldn't help but entertain the despaired thoughts that took off with the starting gun of seeing the sold sticker.

Not only did this put a deluge of a damper on this Christmas, but she also wondered if the magic of this time, this house, this *home* she would ever find again. Probably not. Tears formed saltwater rivers down her cheeks.

All the while, the colored lights continued, oblivious to her broken heart.

Blue. Red. Green. Blue. Red. Green.

Chapter 1

Driving along the meandrous country road that kept relentlessly coming at her like a treadmill, Reilly saw the semi-solid cerulean lake through the bare forest to her right. Cylinders of crisp morning sun strobed at her through the trees. As she hummed along to the Christmas carols on the rental car's satellite radio station, she reminded herself to get satellite radio in her own car back at home in Chicago. Of course, she'd have to get *a car* as well, but that was a minor detail.

Every twenty minutes or so, the baritone-voiced announcer would come on to repeat the station's mantra—*Jingle Radio 191—dedicated to Christmas music 24/7. Yule love it.* Even though Reilly couldn't actually see the spelling of the word, she knew he meant y-u-l-e and appreciated the pun.

She cracked open the driver's side window and drank in a lungful of raw country breeze. It was thick with the scent of pine and winter. The current of air through the car caused the hanging, Christmas tree-shaped air freshener to spin on its string. Reilly giggled to herself as she caught her reflection in the rearview mirror.

She had told everyone who'd had the gall to ask that the Christmas ornament earrings she always kicked off the holiday season with, starting November 1st of course, she wore as more of a joke than anything, to show off the adorably humorous side of her personality.

However, that wasn't entirely true. She was a Christmas aficionado to the core. She also felt holiday-themed jewelry was stylish. And there wasn't just one pair of Christmas earrings in her wardrobe. Sure, it started with the classic silver bulbs, but that quickly escalated to snowman-in-the-snow globe danglers, Christmas tree studs, wreath hoops, and rose gold snowflake Chandelier earrings.

Admittedly, Reilly had gone a little overboard when she'd discovered that AMEX-draining rabbit hole called ETSY. To kick off her Christmas holiday this year, she went with her favorite pair—red heart ornament pendants.

"Proceed to the route," said the electronic GPS, abruptly cutting through the cheerful Christmas carols. Unlike Mr. Baritone of Jingle Radio, this voice had the exact-same stern intonation of an angry teacher who'd just caught you chewing gum in class. Specifically, it sounded much like Reilly's eighth grade math teacher Mrs. Nesserdas. Just the very memory sent spider-crawly chills up Reilly's spine. The woman had all the kindness of a gulag warden.

Reilly thought she remembered hearing that, for a small fee, you could replace that cold voice with a celebrity of your choice. Michael Caine telling you that you were hopelessly lost would be considerably more pleasant. Come to think of it, if only Michael Caine were Reilly's eighth grade math teacher, she might be much better with numbers.

Proceed to the route. She glanced down again at the navigation screen that the smiley guy at the rental place had talked her into getting.

"For only three dollars a day, it's well worth it. Can't put a price on peace of mind."

Well, apparently you could. And it must cost more than three dollars because the thing had no idea where Reilly was. All the screen displayed was a spinning arrow and the word *Searching.* Reilly had only been driving for three hours, but she'd managed to confuse the GPS. Technology was her enemy.

Proceed to the route. Mrs. Nesserdas barked once again. Reilly tapped the screen with her finger—as if that would help. "I can't 'proceed to the route' unless you tell me what the route is."

Reilly's phone rang on her Bluetooth. She didn't have to check the call display. She knew instantly who it was by the ringtone. Her sister, Tara. Ever since the invention of ringtones—a landmark in human innovation, to be sure—Reilly had *Good Vibrations* by Marky Mark and the Funky Bunch tuned to her sister's number whenever she called. It was a long-running joke that had to do with the gigantic teenage crush Tara had on the group's underwear model lead singer for a brief moment, while she was on a momentary break from grunge. In retaliation, whenever Reilly phoned Tara, the ringtone was Ricky Martin's *Livin' la Vida Loca* for similarly embarrassing reasons.

"Did you get there yet?" Tara asked.

Reilly could hear her sister swiveling in her, very expensive, Herman Miller desk chair back in their, even more expensive, top-floor office overlooking Millennium Park. Their office rent was steep. Definitely, more than their fledgling company could afford, presently. But, after all, they had to give their clients the very best impression.

"Who's gonna hire us to stage their house if we can't properly stage our own office?" Reilly had heard her sister ask on many occasions. Hence, purchases like the Herman Miller Aeron chairs, which, granted, were certainly comfortable, but always made Reilly feel as though she was sitting in the captain's chair of the *USS Enterprise,* were deemed necessary. It was in the spirit of this go big or go home philosophy that Tara justified running up her credit card bill, buying Louboutins and other outrageous purchases as work attire.

Reilly, for her part, was more practical—Michael Kors would do just fine. She didn't exactly ascribe to the go big approach and was much more partial to the go home part of that equation than she was even consciously aware of.

"Not yet," Reilly answered her sister as the asphalt belt of the three-dimensional treadmill rolled under the tires of her hired Chevy Cruze. "I'm not even sure there's a *there* there."

Through the phone, Reilly could hear the nose hair-freezing wind blowing upward through the skyscraping corridor of the Chicago metropolis. True to form, the Windy City was living up to its sobriquet.

"I should have just gone with you instead of hanging back a few days." Tara's voice echoed off the walls of the holiday-deserted office.

"Yes, you *should* have. It's Christmas, for Christmas' sake!" Reilly knew that it was these types of Grandma sayings that made Tara question whether they were actually biologically related. It was also for this reason that Reilly tended to use them at any opportunity to get a rise out of her sister.

"Then again," Reilly continued, "You're not exactly a *wilderness*-type person." She heard the clicking of the mouse as Tara multitasked.

"What's that supposed to mean?"

"Your idea of roughing it is IKEA on a Saturday."

"That place is like a casino—no windows, no clocks, and the house always wins. For the record, I'm trying to keep our business afloat."

What the sisters had learned over the past eighteen months was that the home-staging industry was big business and remarkably competitive. It had often left Reilly with that crepuscular three am queasy feeling of having bitten off more than they could chew. She often wondered why those worries always had a knack of rearing their heads in the middle of the night when she was least likely to have anyone to talk her off the ledge, or at the very least, commiserate with her at being on the same ledge. Perhaps it was for precisely that reason the anxieties chose those wee small hours to strike.

"*I'm* committed to continuing our family tradition," Reilly said as she drove blindly, still absent of any directional help from Mrs. Nesserdas, who was still *Searching*… But, somehow, she knew she was going the right way. Maybe it was the fresh smell of the mistletoe coming through the window, though, she didn't actually know what mistletoe smelled like. *Minty?*. Or maybe the fact that she was on a two-lane road, giving her a 50% of being right. Or, maybe again, it was…fate?

"Even if my own family bailed on me this year."

Now, the tone in Tara's voice was a little less playful. "For the *trazillionth* time."

"That's not a real number."

"I am NOT bailing on you. I'll be there in a few days. I'm traveling on Christmas Eve for you—which is the first sign of insanity."

Reilly giggled inwardly. It was so easy to press her little sister's buttons. "I'm not talking about you. Mom and Dad, though." Tara's mouse kept clicking on a morse code shopping spree. "Yeah, they definitely bailed."

"I don't blame them for crossing things off their bucket list."

"Yeah, but *hiking in Papua New Guinea?* That's definitely not on my bucket list," Tara scoffed. "Come to think of it, neither is spending Christmas in a cottage-country town watching some boat parade."

Reilly was aware that Tara knew full well what it was called—the two of them had organized this trip months ago. This was just reverse button-pushing.

As per the Shore Christmas tradition, since childhood each sister—on alternating years—had been allowed to choose where the family would spend the holidays. The girl's parents gave them complete freedom—albeit with two rules: the trip had to be within a reasonable budget, and it couldn't take more than a day to get there. Other than those two caveats, Christmas was always up to Reilly and Tara.

And, with the rotation between the two of them, the polar-opposite taste in the two sisters became obvious. This year, it was no different.

"Annual Christmas Harbor Festival," Reilly corrected. She had been listening to these passive protestations from Tara ever since Reilly had chosen the destination. "Every year, all the boats along the lake are decorated for Christmas. It's what Mistletoe Lake is famous for." Reilly didn't need to explain this to her sister again either. Still, she liked saying it just to arouse her own excitement.

"Mistletoe Lake? We might as well take a trip to Christmas Munchkin Land." Tara's tone had reached a high tide sarcasm.

"Christmas Munchkin Land is next year's trip."

"No, no, no, no, no, no," Tara protested. "Next year is *my* turn. We're going to London."

"Speaking of London. I passed The Sunset Inn on the freeway about five minutes ago. It made the Bates Motel look like the Dorchester. I canceled our reservation. We're not staying there."

"The photos looked good on the website." Tara was obviously still cyber shopping and back to three-quarters listening.

"Well, that must be the first time in history someone has exaggerated on the internet." Reilly could hit a return sarcasm volley over the net when she needed to.

"My sister, the princess."

"Mistletoe Lake is a small town. I'm sure there's a cute B&B or something. I'm so excited!"

"Tell me you're not wearing those Christmas ornament earrings."

Reilly's gaze darted to her reflection in the rearview mirror again. As the two Christmas-red hearts dangled off her ears, she couldn't keep the smile from her voice.

"Me? Christmas ornament earrings? Don't be preposterous."

Reilly practically heard Tara roll her eyes. "Do us a favor—if you see any potential business opportunities before I arrive, *pounce* on them. We need all the help we can get."

Reilly didn't want to entertain any kind of business anxiety right now. "Get back to work, Scrooge."

At that moment, she heard a change in Tara's voice. It was her business voice, devoid of that usual light, jokey lilt. It was also the voice she used when she was concerned about something. Reilly could tell that Tara had clicked off the computer. She now had 100% of her sister's attention, as opposed to the 75% or she'd had before.

"Seriously, though. Are you going to be okay without me for the next few days?"

Not exactly knowing where Tara was going with this, Reilly was slightly taken aback by the question. "Yeah. I *am* a full-grown adult, after all."

"I know. But this is your first Christmas since..." As Tara hesitated, Reilly instantly knew what she was getting at. The reason for that silky concern in her voice. Reilly mouthed the word along with her as she finally said it. "Darly."

Reilly's ex, Greg Darlington, whom all her family and friends warmly referred to as Darly. It was a nickname that everyone used, except Reilly. She just called him Greg. Gregory when she was angry. The two had been together for four-and-a-half years. Everybody loved Darly. Everyone was heartbroken when they split up, particularly Reilly's parents. Almost as much as Reilly was.

"Greg and I broke up *eight months ago,*" Reilly said, a tinge defensively.

"I know."

Tara sounded as though she were the older wiser sister, which she wasn't. Okay, maybe wiser in some ways but never older. That was indisputable.

"But this will be your first Christmas since the fall of *Greilly*."

Another imposed nickname that Reilly never used and wasn't at all fond of. She always thought it sounded like an ogre character in some off-brand fairy tale.

"I just wanna make sure you're okay," Tara continued.

Reilly hadn't really thought about it. Or perhaps she'd driven the thoughts from her head before they could lay root there, like weeds. But Tara was right. This *would* be the first Christmas in five years she wouldn't be spending with Greg. Thinking about that made her heart pang with sadness.

She let her mind briefly wander into that labyrinth of heartache and wondered how he was spending his Christmas this year. Probably at his brother's place in San Diego. She hoped he was doing okay. Since the split, they'd made the mutual agreement not to be in contact. It was easier that way. By an infinitesimal amount, but still. Before Reilly could allow herself the next question—*had he met anyone?*—she turned and walked right out of the mental maze, knowing that if she got too far in, she might not find her way out.

"I'm totally fine."

"Are you sure? Because you can't even seem to find your way to this backwater town by yourself."

It was at this moment Mrs. Nesserdas reared her ugly voice again. *Proceed to the route.*

Tara cackled. "Busted."

"I'll call you when I get there."

"*If* you get there."

"Goodbye." As Reilly ended the call, she couldn't resist letting her mind swirl with thoughts of Greg. She sincerely hoped he was having a good Christmas. She loved him. And if he'd met someone, she'd be happy. Also sad. *Love is a paradox.*

Suddenly, the interminable highway that she'd been travelling on came to an end. As she brought the car to a stop, Reilly found that she was at a fork in the road. As Mrs. Nesserdas' satellite was still of no help, it was left to Reilly to make a guess. She eeny-meeny-miney-mo'ed it and decided on left. As she took the turn, Reilly cranked up the Christmas carols and hoped she'd made the right decision.

Chapter 2

Reilly drew in an awestruck mini breath as her eyes soaked in the panorama of what appeared to be a painting come to life. As she navigated the last curve in the road, past the icicled trees standing sentry, breaking through the milky mist, there it was: a picturesque hamlet nestled on the edge of a looking-glass, indigo lake. She decided there and then that when she recounted this story later in life, she most certainly would include the fabricated detail of moving through the fog into that enchanting realm.

She'd also tell her grandchildren that she'd felt as though she wasn't driving—that her Avis loaner had suddenly gained autonomy and was taking her by its own volition to the place she was *supposed* to be. That second part, though fantastical, wasn't entirely made up. Reilly did feel as though she wasn't in complete control of the car. Some part of it may have been driving itself.

Arriving on the town's quaint Main Street, Reilly passed a handcrafted wooden sign that read: *Welcome to Mistletoe Lake, pop. 1119*. She wondered what they did when a resident either was born or died or immigrated or emigrated, altering that quite specific population number. Beneath that, in a slightly smaller wood-carved font, the sign read: *Home of the World-Famous Christmas Harbor Festival*. She smiled to herself.

"We officially have a *there*."

She stepped out of the car and did a three-sixty of her surroundings. The old-timey streetlamps were crisscrossed with colored lights, culminating in a large pine tree at the end of the street in the town's main square and was serving its seasonal role as the communal Christmas tree. The glorious evergreen was decorated trunk-to-top with ornaments that appeared to be hand placed, Reilly imagined, by the young local inhabitants hoisted up on the shoulders of their parents to reach the highest branch possible. That being a barometer for how much the kids had grown from the previous year.

The ornaments that were too high for even parental assistance must have been placed with help of the local fire department cherry picker bucket, the very same one they likely used to get cats out of trees.

With the freshly fallen snow blanketing everything, softly muffling all sound, everywhere Reilly looked was an image of warm invitation. A barber shop, a mom-and-pop diner, and a red-brick library. In the middle of the town square was a general store, right out of a Thornton Wilder play.

Before, when anyone would refer to something as Rockwellian, Reilly would never be able to connect with the reference. She had always categorized Rockwell art in the same class as stuff you'd find leftover and unsold at the end of a garage sale, alongside the VHS cassettes and chipped vases. It was probably an overly harsh judgment, Reilly knew. But she hadn't gotten what the attraction was. However, now being submerged into the pastoral authenticity of Mistletoe Lake complete with the line-up of boats along the harbor, she finally got it. This town was undeniably Rockwellian.

Reilly was drawn toward the general store, where a sign in the window boasted, *Visitor Information Here*.

As she entered the establishment festooned with holiday cheer, Reilly could tell it was a one-stop shop for anything a person could need. There was local farm-grown produce and homemade confectioneries, including a freezer full of

pies made from every conceivable berry type. A sign stuck
to the freezer's glass door read *Mag's Pies*, which was a sim-
ple-yet-brilliant stroke of marketing genius. Though Reilly
had a feeling the pun was purely unintentional. There were
hardware supplies, bait, fishing lines, and even a newsstand
that, surprisingly, carried a copy of the Sunday New York
times. It was from two Sundays ago, but still…

An entire corner of the store was dedicated to selling
tchotchkes, which Reilly had always thought sounded like
the name of a Russian playwright. The knick-knacks were
themed around the town's unusual, yet catchy, name. There
was a rack full of emerald-green, mass-produced t-shirts that
read, *Kiss Me, I went to Mistletoe Lake*, red and green knitted
footy socks called *Mistletoes*, buttons, mugs, bumper stickers—you name it. One thing was for sure: some small-town
hero went to business school and brought those marketing
skills back with them.

"Do you work here?" Reilly hadn't really registered many
details about the guy standing behind the counter where
she'd asked the question. Perhaps it was the kaleidoscope of
other stuff competing for her attention.

He certainly wasn't the kind of person who faded into
the scenery. Yet, at the same time, there was nothing flashy
about him. He was averagely tall, with wavy, khaki-brown
hair. He had a boyish face, but years of outdoor living had
balanced him out to looking his age—which was probably
just shy of forty. He wore a flannel shirt and faded jeans, and
by their well-loved condition, it was obvious that he wore
them often. His aura was at once cagey yet openly inviting,
like a wild animal who wasn't sure he could trust you but
wanted to.

As the guy focused on Reilly, the hint of an almost imperceptible grin played on his face, and his eyes crinkled.
"It's an odd question to ask, isn't it? Considering I'm standing behind the counter."

Reilly couldn't tell if the guy was playing around or being a jerk, which made him all the more interesting. She smiled with slight embarrassment. "Right. Of course. Silly me."

She took a breath, realizing she was flustered. Why was she flustered? She'd come into the store because of the *Visitor Information Here* sign in the window. She was a visitor, and she needed information. Pretty straightforward.

The critical voice in her head that liked to pop up in situations like these told her to *get it together*. Yet, there was a curious tingling feeling working its way up from the end of her toes.

Reilly instantly felt self-conscious about the silly Christmas earrings she was wearing. *What? Now they're silly?* Perhaps it was her noticing the tacky tourist trinkets in the corner of the store that set her off. Not wanting to be grouped into the same kitschy category, as the guy looked back down at his newspaper, Reilly very subtly took the earrings off and stuffed them in her pocket.

"Well, I was actually wondering—" she continued before being cut off again.

"Actually, I don't though." The guy looked up from his paper. He was still completely deadpan, but that microscopic grin had grown twenty percent.

"You don't…" That tingling feeling had now made its way to the base of her spine.

"Work here," the guy clarified. With the glint in his eyes giving off a flirtatious vibe, Reilly decided to respond with some sass of her own.

"Well, if you *don't* work here, you probably shouldn't be behind the counter, should you?"

At this, his lips broke into a full-on smile. "I suppose you're right." He gave Reilly a quick, sizing-up glance.

"You from the city?"

Reilly smirked. There was no turning back, now. "*The* city? You know that there are more than one, right?"

"I've heard that," he said, "but I don't much believe it. Next, you'll try to convince me that the Earth isn't flat."

Reilly burst out laughing. Point, set, match for flannel shirt guy.

She tried to *force* herself not to look at his left hand—specifically the ring finger. That's something that Tara would make no bones about doing. Reilly was more subtle. But she couldn't stop herself. At least if she *had* to look, she hoped she wouldn't be too obvious about it. However, she failed on both accounts. She looked, and he saw her looking. *Oh, well.*

The upside was that there was no ring. *That doesn't mean anything,* said that critical voice. And what did she care, anyway? She was just a visitor looking for information, right?

"You got me. I am, in fact, from THE city," replied Reilly.

"Well, I hate to disappoint you, but they're all out of butter tarts. Should be making more in a few days."

Reilly looked at him blankly. "Butter tarts?" By his reaction, Reilly could tell that this was something many people came into this store looking for.

"Christmas nutmeg butter tarts. They're always a big hit with the Seasonals."

Once again, Reilly stared at him with puzzled blankness. "*Seasonals?*"

"Yeah, you know. Tourists."

She hadn't exactly thought of herself as a tourist. After all, she wasn't there to snap selfies for her Instagram page. She had wished there could be a more appropriate title for what she was doing in Mistletoe Lake.

Explorer implied she was there to pilfer land and co-opt culture. *Wanderer* sounded way too hippy-dippy. Despite the sign in the window, *Visitor* suggested an alien from another planet. *Tourist* she'd reluctantly accept. But it seemed as though she'd already been labeled a *Seasonal*.

Before she could explain that her question *wasn't* about butter tarts, though, now that he'd mentioned it, they *did* sound interesting, the doorbell rang again as someone else entered the store. It was a young girl, probably twelve-years-old, Reilly guessed. Her arms were full of what looked like Christmas decorations.

As the girl approached the counter, she said to Reilly's flirt-sparring partner, "Thanks for minding the store," and before she completed her sentence with the word *dad*, Reilly knew they were related. Same eyes, same hair.

It was only when she had gotten almost within arm's reach of them did the girl register Reilly's presence. In fact, Reilly could tell that there was something that *made* her really notice Reilly. Perhaps she, too, sensed this inexplicable gravitational pull between Reilly and her dad.

Her brisk gait instantly slowed to an immediate stop, like a cat who's suddenly heard an unrecognized noise.

"No problem, honey," said the guy. As he made his way around the counter, he flashed Reilly his crooked smile. "Hope you enjoy your stay."

Reilly smiled back. "I'll do my best." She noticed the girl watched this exchange with the attentiveness of a tennis match spectator. Reilly thought that she saw a pleased glimmer in her eyes, but she could have been imagining it.

The doorbell clanged again, and the guy was gone. The girl went over to the empty display window and put her decorations beside it. She looked over at Reilly with new eyes, but her businesslike demeanor had returned.

"You visiting?"

Reilly nodded.

"Well, we're all out of—"

"—butter tarts. I heard." Reilly watched the girl carefully unpack the decorations. "Are you the one who decorated the store?" For some inexplicable reason, Reilly felt the need to get on the good side of the daughter. Actually, it was explicable. She knew very well why.

Because I have a crush on her dad. She'd only been in this store all of five minutes. *How fast do crushes happen?*

The girl gazed at the pile of decorations and nodded. "My dad's not really into decorating for Christmas this year so this is my only outlet. The finishing touch is a display for the window."

The decorations weren't the typical fare. Instead of garland and ornaments, there were toy boats, dozens of LED lights, and miniature model trees. The eccentric collection piqued Reilly's curiosity.

"I want to do a model of the Mistletoe Lake Christmas Harbor Festival," the girl said, obviously anticipating Reilly's confusion. Reilly took a step closer. The kid was staring at the window like a surgeon deciding where to make the first cut.

"I'm really excited to be in town for the festival." Hearing herself, Reilly decided she sounded like she was trying too hard and decided to dial up the cool. "Is it true that every boat in the harbor goes all out in lights and decorations?"

The girl smiled. "Yep. It's really beautiful." Then, the smile faded somewhat. "Well, all the boats except one."

Reilly heard the sadness in her tone but thought better of asking about it. Instead, she changed gears. "Do you know if there's a hotel or a B&B in town?"

The girl raised a dubious eyebrow. "There's only one B&B in Mistletoe Lake, but it's probably fully booked because of Christmas."

So why hadn't said B&B come up on her web search months ago when she was planning the trip? Did they not have a website? Surely, they weren't that hardcore old-fashioned.

"You could go over and try your luck." She continued. "My grandmother runs it."

Chapter 3

The silver-haired woman looked up from behind the reception desk at the Mistletoe Lake Bed and Breakfast as Reilly entered.

"How may I help you?"

The well-worn Persian-rugged and wallpapered lobby was perfumed with a bouquet of a wood-burning fire and wafts of homemade goodness from the kitchen. "Hi...I was sent here by your granddaughter." Reilly once again unintentionally adopted that Sorry-I'm-a-tourist tone.

At the mention of her granddaughter, the woman smiled. "Emma."

"Yes, Emma. She told me to come by to see if you had any rooms available." Seeing the apologetic muscle contractions on the woman's face made Reilly feel foolish. *Of course, they didn't have a room. It's Christmas, dummy.*

"I'm terribly sorry, but we're completely full." Reilly could tell that she was *actually* sorry, too. "Christmas is our peak season," the kind, grandmotherly woman continued, "due to the—"

"—Harbor Festival." Reilly politely finished her sentence. "That's kinda why I'm here." *Then why didn't you make a reservation?* That critical voice in Reilly's head didn't like to relinquish the bully pulpit sometimes.

"We book out months in advance." A conciliatory smile accompanied the explanation. "I could try The Sunset Inn for you and see if they have something available."

Reilly thanked her and privately hoped that the decrepit motel she was too snobby to stay in not an hour earlier still had a room available. Any port in a Christmas Harbor Festival storm.

As Emma's grandmother went to the phone, Reilly looked over at the adjoining room, the lounge, she assumed, where she could hear periodic pops of a fire. Along with the quiet clink of teacups being replaced on their saucer counterparts and the ever-so-faint sound of classical music, it was a peaceful harmony of hominess.

With the same blanketing feeling of warmth she experienced when she first arrived in town, Reilly had the sensation of belonging. And, giving in to a rare fairy tale notion, she somehow just *knew* that the kindly proprietor would return to say that there had been a miraculous cancellation in Reilly's favor. Because it was Christmas. Things like that happened at Christmas.

"I'm sorry." The woman returned with another apologetic look. "The Sunset Inn just gave away their last room. It's a busy time for the whole area."

Reilly smiled as her fairy tale wish evaporated like a raindrop on a hot skillet. "Just my luck. Thank you for your help."

The lady then politely excused herself. "I've got to get the scones out of the oven."

Scones. That's what the smell was. Reilly sighed. So now she had nowhere to stay. *Great.*

With the realization of her predicament slowly descending like a thick fog, Reilly was drawn into the next room— the lounge—where covering one wall were dozens of framed black and white photographs. As Reilly got a closer look, she saw that they were all of past Mistletoe Lake Harbor Festival winners, each image depicting the beamingly happy first-place recipients victoriously standing on the decks of their decorated boats.

Beneath each photo was a small brass plaque displaying the year, going back decades. Reilly marveled at an entire era of the town's history displayed before her.

At the very top of the exhibit, one particular photo caught Reilly's eye, a shot depicting an ear-to-ear smiling little boy with what appeared to be his father. As Reilly's eyes took in the details of the image, letting it transport her mind there, a voice from behind brought her back to the present.

"It's nice, but the decor is a bit dated, isn't it?" In that infinitesimally fast way the human brain can be, Reilly searched through her memory trying to place that voice. She recognized it. But it couldn't be someone she knew. *Not here.*

Reilly turned around to see...Edward Louis. She had to take a moment to make sure that her eyes weren't playing tricks on her. She blinked, and he was still standing there, his spray-tanned face grinning back at her.

"Hello, Reilly Shore!"

Reilly couldn't believe it. *What on Earth was Edward Louis doing here?*

She and Tara had met Edward Louis exactly fourteen and a half months ago. She remembered the date because it was her birthday—October 6th. She was supposed to have been doing her very favorite thing that night: tacos, margaritas, and karaoke at *Ole! Guacamole!* It was an annual birthday tradition.

However, on the previous birthday, her taco festivities had to be shifted to another night because a monkey wrench had been thrown into her plans. A monkey wrench named Tara. On the same night of Reilly's birthday, there had been another, more importantly pressing engagement for the sisters to attend. Well, more importantly pressing *to Tara,* anyway.

There had been a book launch taking place that night. Reilly really didn't go in for any kind of launch, save for perhaps one that took place at Cape Canaveral, and even then, probably not. This was a book launch for an actress whose name Reilly couldn't remember. This was the type of event that would rank behind unanesthetized dental surgery for her on any night of the year, but *especially* on her birthday. However, Tara insisted they go.

It was smack in the middle of this social calamity the sisters had met Edward Louis. At first, Reilly couldn't take him even 2% seriously. He was nice enough but had a gameshow host quality that Reilly found off-putting. As the three engaged in small talk, Reilly had eyed her sister, wordlessly reprimanding her for what she was thinking. And Reilly knew very well what it was—*this guy could be good for business.*

She had doubted that Edward would come through as a legitimate potential customer when Tara handed him their brand-new embossed business card. She didn't even believe him when he visited their newly leased, still partially unpacked office the next day. But, after staging four of his properties within the last year, Reilly had to concede that it was probably worth shifting her birthday celebrations to another night.

Over the past year, Edward Louis had begun to grow on Reilly. All those initially annoying qualities became enduring quirks. Despite having a more-dollars-than-sense taste and mannequinesque style, he had a good heart underneath. She charitably decided that he was just a bit insecure and dealing with it in the best way he could.

Still, seeing Edward in this cottage country B&B was utterly incongruous, like seeing a rhinoceros on the subway.

"Edward…what are you doing here?" She stammered, trying not to make the surprise in her voice sound like an unpleasant shock. Though the unexpected colliding of her business world with her Christmas vacation did make her feel slightly that way.

The two hugged their hellos, giving Reilly a nose full of that Italian cologne Edward always wore too much of. "I'm here because of you!" he said, still grinning.

"Me?" The mental effort of trying to catch up was giving Reilly the equivalent of an ice cream headache.

Edward nodded proudly. "I was in your office a few months ago when you were planning this trip for your...what do you call it? Yearly holiday custom?

"Annual Christmas tradition," Reilly corrected robotically.

"Yeah, that's it," he said with a finger snap. "You were researching Mistletoe Lake, and you inspired me to check it out."

She vaguely remembered Edward dropping by the office one day in the fall for a cappuccino and remarking on Reilly's research for their Christmas destination.

"This town is *incredible*." Edward continued, with overly enthusiastic volume. "I've already convinced my sister and her kids to come later this week."

Reilly couldn't help but wonder whether he was staying in the B&B room that might have been hers.

"How's business these days?"

Reilly shrugged, "Oh, you know, just plugging along." It wasn't exactly a lie. They *were* plugging along. Some days it was like plugging leaks in a sinking ship but plugging, nonetheless.

"I've got to tell you again just how talented you are. The way you staged that last townhouse for me is the reason it sold as quickly as it did. And a bidding war to boot!"

Reilly shrugged again, this time with a modest blush. She remembered that property well. Much of the effort went into politely saving Edward from his own questionable taste. "It was a good location. It was bound to sell, regardless," she white-lied.

Edward wasn't having it. "It was a lousy location and a dump. Still, I did very well because of you." He glanced at his watch. The thing was the size of a hockey puck. "I should run. I've got an appointment."

Of course, he does. Only Edward Louis could have an appointment on his Christmas vacation.

"Since we're both in town let's meet for lunch. I'd love to catch up." He gave Reilly another Italian cologne hug and strode away.

In the silence once again, the fireplace crackled at her.

Chapter 4

Reilly walked slowly along Mistletoe Lake's Main Street, back to her car. It was the aimless shuffle of a person unsure of where to go. As a rule, she didn't get stressed out about things like this. She was a believer in the worldview her parents fostered within her. Everything happens for a reason and always works out for the best. But this was a predicament. It was almost comical. There was a solution; she just hadn't found it yet.

As Reilly approached her car, she saw the General Store where Emma had made considerable progress on the display window. It drew Reilly inside.

As the doorbell announced Reilly's re-entrance into the store, Emma looked up from her opus.

"Any luck?" she asked, with a look that said she already knew the answer. Reilly shook her head. "So…what are you going to do?"

Reilly felt as though the adult-kid roles were reversed. "I Googled some nearby places. How far is Suttondale?"

"About three hours."

Reilly deflated even further. That wasn't going to work.

In a subconscious effort to distract herself from thinking about her complete lack of options, she transferred her gaze to Emma's work on the window. The mise-en-scene was coming along well. "This looks fantastic. You're quite the artist."

The girl grinned with pride. "Thank you. I'm just having a little trouble executing the scope of my vision, though."

"Well…if you'd like a hand, I'm happy to offer one. It is kinda what I do for a living. And I've got nowhere to go."

Emma's eyes lit up. Her tween excitement took over. "That would be amazing!" She extended her hand. "My name's Emma. People call me Em."

"Mine's Reilly."

Over the next hour and a half, the two new fast friends sat in the window of the General Store, ensconced in the undertaking of the project. Through the process, Reilly played the role of diligent assistant, like a sous-chef working under a Michelin-Star maestro, following the young girl's instructions to a T.

The two carefully stuck the tiny LED lights onto the miniature toy boats, used white-out to paint snow onto the model pine trees, and carefully poured water into the basin in the window, filling up the Lilliputian doppelganger of Mistletoe Lake.

As they worked away, something grabbed ahold of Reilly's heart. A warm feeling, like that first sip of wine. *This was fun.* A kind of fun she hadn't remembered having in a while.

As a finishing touch, they hung a glow-in-the-dark half-moon over the tiny lake.

"Gotta say, you've got serious talent." This time, the compliment from Reilly was more peer-to-peer than adult-to-kid.

"Thanks. My dream is to become a set designer. I want to work on Broadway someday. I applied to this private art school in New Hampshire. It's one of the best in the country. I really hope I get in."

Reilly didn't think of herself as necessarily old in any way but sitting next to this kid with stars in her eyes and everything in front of her, made her feel positively ancient. As though she'd lost something of herself. It was a sensation that had been bubbling up from her subconscious on occasion recently.

"Well, if it were up to me, you'd be a shoo-in," Reilly said, aware that it sounded like one of those head-patting placations you say to a younger person. But she truly meant it.

"You said this is kinda what you do for a living. You're a designer as well?"

"Yeah. Interior design. That's what I'm trained in, anyway. But now my sister and I have a home-staging business."

Emma looked at her with puzzlement. "What's home-staging?"

"Sometimes people buy vacant houses so they can fix them up and sell them for more money." That explanation always sounded quite straightforward to Reilly. It was this next part that always came off a little hollow. "So, they hire people like me to decorate the empty houses and make them look homier. That way they can charge a higher price."

A moment passed. Emma nodded, seeming to understand, or *pretending* to anyway. Then another confused look crossed the girl's face, and she changed the subject. "How come you're spending Christmas alone?"

Reilly was knocked on her heels a little by the innocent forwardness of the question, though she tried to play it cool. "I'm not *technically* spending it alone. My sister is meeting me here toward the end of the week."

"What about your boyfriend or husband or something?"

Reilly couldn't stop herself from chuckling, out of embarrassment, sure, but also in appreciation of the kid's authenticity.

A mortified look crossed Emma's face. "Sorry. Was that a rude question to ask?"

Reilly shook her head. "Not at all. You just remind me of myself when I was your age." She considered how to give the girl a properly sufficient answer. "I don't have a boyfriend or husband or something. At the moment." A lightning flash of Greg ricocheted through her mind.

"Why not?" Emma pressed. "You seem like a catch."

I'm not going to get off easy here. If Emma weren't so artistically gifted, she might have considered a career as a lawyer. "I guess…I'm just waiting for the right guy to come along." Reilly wasn't sure if she truly meant that or if it was just something that was programmed into every single person's head.

Emma was struggling with Reilly's response as well. "You don't strike me as the kind of person who's waiting for a guy to come along."

Man, this girl and her diamond laser wisdom. And in that single moment, she knew she and Emma would become friends.

"You're right." Reilly was both impressed at the insight and flattered at the compliment. "Maybe, I'm…" she searched for the most accurate answer, "…keeping my eyes open for the right guy to come along."

At this, Emma nodded with satisfied approval. "Smart."

Another moment passed. Emma glanced at her new friend for a sizing-up beat, as though contemplating something of boundless gravity. Then she finally asked, "You wanna come to my dad's boat for some coconut milk eggnog?"

Reilly could tell that this was an invitation of high privilege. She was flattered. Also, literally had nowhere else to go. "Coconut milk eggnog? How could I say no?"

Chapter 5

Mistletoe Lake stretched blue out to the horizon. It was marbled with silvery patches of ice and dotted with sporadic, castaway islands in the distance. The sharp, wet, breeze off the ocean-like body of water filled Reilly's lungs and gave her a yin-yang sensation with the cold air against the warmth of her body.

Moored on the wooden harbor along the looping shoreline were over a dozen gleaming boats. All the vessels appeared to be quite new, and each was in various stages of decorations— clearly in preparation for the upcoming harbor festival. All the boats except one, which was grinch-like in that it was devoid of any holiday cheer.

As Reilly followed Emma along the pier, she figured she was being led toward that very boat. It wasn't a prediction worthy of Nostradamus exactly as the vessel's name was printed in large black letters across the cream-white hull— *The Emma.*

Despite its lack of Christmas spangle, the vessel still managed to stand out next to its more hulking, newer model counterparts. Reilly snapped a single frame image of it in her mind's eye and thought that with a little sepia tone, it could be a portrait of a scene out of 1960s Hyannis Port.

Getting closer, she recognized a familiar figure in a flannel shirt standing on the boat's deck. Emma's dad. Just for fun, she silently tried to guess his name. Had to be Jack, Tom, or something similarly utilitarian. He looked like the kind of guy who had a name to match his personality. Dave? Mike?

As the two stepped up the gangplank, Reilly wasn't exactly sure that was what it was called since it sounded more like something to do with pirates, she was taken by the cherry wood, mirror-varnished chrome finish of the boat. It was in immaculate condition and gave Reilly the feeling of being in a floating version of a vintage car.

Seeing Reilly, Emma's dad—Jake? Brad?—smiled with easy charm. He didn't seem to be particularly surprised to see her, as if he knew their paths would somehow cross again. Though, how could he have? For all he knew, Reilly was just another Seasonal passing through town looking for butter tarts. Perhaps in some small, subconscious part of his mind, he knew he'd see her again. Reilly assumed this because she'd felt the same way the first time they'd met.

"Dad, this is a new friend of mine," Emma said proudly. "You two met earlier."

He wiped his engine-greasy hands with a rag. "Not officially.

City Girl, right?" He asked with a playful expression.

Reilly got a momentary glimpse behind his cool demeanor. He seemed a little nervous, too, which he covered with teasing.

"I also respond to Reilly." She tried to match his playful tone. "Shall I call you Country Boy?"

"If you like. Ray works, too."

Ray. Of course. That was certainly in the orbit of names she had guessed for him. And it fit perfectly.

Ray finally took Reilly's hand, and they shook. His skin was work-worn, like an old leather glove, but his grip was gentle.

"Sorry my hands are dirty," Ray said. "Been fixing up the boat."

As far as Reilly could tell, the boat didn't seem in need of much fixing up. And the level of dirt on his hands was the very last thing on her mind.

After a moment, Emma asked, "You want some eggnog, Dad?"

With an ever-so-slight lingering look at Reilly, he said, "Love some." Then added, "As long as it's not the healthy stuff."

"*Healthier* stuff. And it is," Emma corrected, with parental matter-of-factness.

"My daughter is trying to turn me into a vegan." Ray playfully rolled his eyes. It was pride masquerading as a complaint.

"My so-hard-done-by dad doesn't appreciate me helping him make better diet choices." This incessant teasing seemed to run in the family.

As Emma went into the boat's cabin, Reilly and Ray were left alone. Reilly's face flushed. She hoped he didn't notice.

Pull it together. Besides this Ray fellow isn't anything near the type of guy you've been romantically involved with before. At least, amongst the three-and-a-half significant relationships she'd had in her adult life—Charles, Darren, Peter, and finally, Greg in chronological order. They were all academics, played things like golf and squash, and all seemed middle-aged before they were middle-aged. Plus, not one flannel shirt in the bunch.

Besides, Reilly had no idea what Ray's relationship status was.

For all she knew, some no make-up, just-woke-up-like-this knockout could walk out at any moment and introduce herself as Ray's girlfriend. Looking for something to distract from her utter awkwardness, Reilly glanced around the boat, noticing a framed photo. It was the very same black and white image of the little boy and his father she'd seen in the B&B.

Ray noticed Reilly noticing it. "That's me and my dad. This was his boat."

Reilly saw another almost imperceptible gearshift of emotion behind Ray's eyes. He wasn't a guy who could easily hide what he was feeling. She found it endearing. And refreshing. She'd had her fill of men who were enigmatic to the point of being aloof. She'd also registered Ray's use of the past tense when referring to his father but thought better of asking.

"It's gorgeous." It wasn't simply the exquisite craftsmanship that she was referring to. There was also a feeling she got by being there. An inexplicable sensation of comfort. *Belonging?*

Emma returned from the cabin with three cups of eggnog. *Coconut milk* eggnog. Reilly could taste the hint of tropical sweetness. Since the little girl wasn't followed by any girlfriend of Ray's, Reilly became a little more optimistic that such a person didn't exist after all.

Emma had a twinkling, mischievous look on her face as she took her first sip of eggnog. "Dad, Reilly is visiting for Christmas, but she doesn't have anywhere to stay. Aaaaaaannnnd." She stretched out the word for dramatic effect. "I've just had the most brilliant idea ever."

"I always get a little nervous when you say that, Em."

Curiosity warred with nerves in Reilly's stomach. *Where was the kid going with this?*

Undeterred, Emma continued with a flourish, like a magician showing the audience that she *hadn't* actually sawed the volunteer from the audience in half. "Reilly should stay here!"

Hearing this, Reilly was mortified. The last thing she'd want was for Ray to think she'd engineered this. A pushy opportunistic tourist who'd befriended a kid in order to weasel herself into a place to stay. She'd prefer to sleep in the car than have Ray think that of her.

"Here?" Both Reilly and Ray said simultaneously, like hammy actors in a bad sitcom.

Oblivious to the awkwardness she'd caused in both adults, Emma cheerfully continued. "Yes! My dad and I stay at a cottage in town. The boat just sits empty at night. Think of it like a floating Airbnb."

The girl did make a convincing argument, but Reilly wasn't sure it was a good idea. By his face, neither was Ray.

"I-I wouldn't dream of imposing," Reilly stammered.

"Don't be silly." Emma made things even more awkward. "You have no other option."

The girl was right. It was hard to turn the offer down. Even if it wasn't official, yet. She turned to Ray.

"I can pay," she said, with further embarrassment.

Ray looked at Reilly, and for the first time in the very brief few hours they'd known each other, his face was unreadable. Reilly assumed he was searching his brain for an excuse that was plausible but not rude. Finally, he said, "We don't take money from visitors who are in a bind. That's not our style around here."

In that moment, all of Reilly's suspicions that Ray was a good guy were confirmed.

"Well, if you're fixing up the boat," she offered, "at least let me earn my keep."

Ray spiked his eyebrows. "You know anything about inboard motors?"

"A little. If they're anything like car engines. I used to help my dad tune up the car before family road trips when I was a kid."

"And she's *really* good at Christmas decorations." Emma piped in, a continuing locomotive of enthusiasm.

"Remember what we talked about, though?" Ray said to Emma, a cautioning tone entering his voice. "We're probably not going to be decorating the boat this year. That buyer seems interested. He said that he's going to make his decision very soon."

As Emma did her very best to underplay her disappointment surrounding this topic, Reilly was acutely aware of her third-wheel status in this family moment.

"I know," Emma said with a pinch of defeat in her voice, "but, just in case."

Ray took a conceding breath. It was obvious that more than anything, he was a concerned dad who would do anything not to break his daughter's heart. "Okay, honey. Just in case." He glanced over at Reilly. He'd made his decision, even though his daughter had made it *for* him already. "You're welcome to stay here on the boat, but obviously, only until the sale." He then added, "We have to sell our boat as quickly as possible."

"I understand." There was a sudden buzz of elation in her stomach. "Thank you."

Ray's only response was a smile. She wondered if he wanted to see her again as much as she wanted to see him.

With the grin of someone who has victoriously executed a secret plan, Emma giddily bounced to her feet. "I'll come help you with your luggage!"

Chapter 6

"So, you just agreed to stay on a stranger's boat?"

Facetime only enhanced Tara's judgmental incredulity. She was out of breath as she simultaneously cycled on her Peloton. Tara just wouldn't be Tara if she wasn't multitasking.

"I know it sounds crazy. But I slept more soundly last night than I have in a long time. Must have been a combination of the water gently lapping against the boat, or the comforting country silence." Reilly replied over the whirl of the spin bike.

Sitting on the boat's deck with the bed's duvet wrapped around her, she drank in the golden morning view of the lake. "I can't explain it. I just immediately felt at home here."

"Well, I'm not staying on some old boat." Tara mopped the sweat off her face. "I get seasick."

"Now, who's being a princess?" Reilly sipped the cup of coffee she'd scrounged together from various abandoned items in the boat's tiny kitchen.

"You'll never guess who I ran into in town yesterday."

"Bigfoot."

"Edward Louis."

Tara immediately stopped pedaling. Now fully focused on Reilly, her eyes illuminated with excitement. "Edward *one-*

of-our-best-clients-ever Louis? He's in *Mistletoe Lake*? What are the chances? What's he doing there?"

It was the machine gun fire of questions that Tara did whenever she sensed an opportunity, professional or personal. In this case, it was both.

"He must be planning some big business deal!"

Even with the slow, glitchy Wi-Fi connection, Reilly could see the wheels turning in her sister's head even faster than the ones on the Peloton had been going. "Or," Reilly tempered, Tara's wont to jump to conclusions, "he's just taking a Christmas holiday." Reilly's eyes narrowed. "Did you know he was going to be here?"

Tara adopted an innocent expression. "Me? How would I know?"

Of the two of them, Tara had corresponded with Edward more with consistent random messages just to constantly keep on his radar. It wouldn't be beneath her to pull the puppet strings and have him coincidentally spend Christmas in the very same town as they were. But Reilly believed Tara when she said she had nothing to do with the coincidence. Had she orchestrated something so devious, she would have been unable to stop herself from bragging about it.

"You should take a meeting with him!" Tara had completely abandoned her morning ride.

"Yeah, I'm sure that's *exactly* what he wants." Reilly spit out a coffee grind that had made it into her cup. "For me to corner him on his Christmas vacation and shake him down for business."

"I'll do it if you're too proud."

And she would, too. After all, Tara was the one who'd ended up collecting from the subscribers on Reilly's paper route. And she did it with all the relish of an auditor from the Internal Revenue Service.

"A solid contract to start the year is exactly what we need."

Tara wasn't wrong about that. Every month, the bills were coming in like a meteor shower.

"Edward is a nice guy and everything, but he's got *terrible* taste." Reilly pleaded. "Remember he had us stucco over those gorgeous, exposed brick walls in that townhouse?" Reilly nearly shuddered at the thought.

They had talked him out of a lot of poor decisions, but they couldn't talk him out of that one. Their dad had an expression about things like that— "It was like pouring ginger ale into twelve-year-old Scotch." Reilly had never liked Scotch. It tasted like drinking a bag of peat moss to her, but the metaphor was dead-on.

"Don't be such an artist. Be *professional,"* Tara said, hanging a lantern on the opportunistic divide between her and her sister.

"Did Edward happen to say if he was seeing anyone? Any mention of a girlfriend?" She made a show of preparing her post-workout smoothie in her Vitamix, a clear attempt to distract from the very obvious reason for her question.

"No. He just mentioned that his sister and her kids were spending the holidays with him."

"How 'bout a wedding ring?" Tara asked between loud frappes of fruit and protein powder.

Reilly rolled her eyes. "You've got the hots for Edward, and you're telling *me* to be professional? Tara, he's a client."

"I don't have the hots for him. I'm just curious. Besides, even if I did, we young people have mastered the art of mixing business and pleasure, unlike your generation." The generation Tara referred to consisted of the nineteen months Reilly had on her. "Does he still look as handsome as ever?"

"I'm hanging up now."

Just as Reilly ended the call and was taking in the panoramic view of the peaceful lake, a familiar voice called from the dock.

"Permission to come aboard?" Ray wore a different but strikingly similar, faded flannel shirt. *So, he does have more than one.*

As he stepped up onto the deck, Reilly made a subtle attempt at straightening out her bedhead and hoped the pillow creases in her face had ironed themselves out. She hadn't been expecting Ray to come by so early and was caught off-guard.

He gave her an apologetic look. "I hope it's not too early to disturb you. I'd love to get some work done on this engine."

Despite her appearance, Reilly was happy to see him. "Of course. No disturbance at all."

His gaze darted to Reilly's cup. "You managed to make coffee? I was gonna offer to pick you up one in town."

"I found some grounds in the freezer. With the leftover eggnog and using a paper towel as a filter, I MacGyvered myself a latte. You want one?"

Ray nodded, clearly impressed with her resourcefulness. "Sure."

As Reilly fixed him a cup in the boat's closet-sized kitchen, which consisted of a bar fridge, a hot plate, and an 80s-era microwave that was as dainty as a large cement safe, she heard odd grunts and groans coming from below the deck.

As she poked her head into the engine room, she found Ray on his hands and knees struggling with a wrench under the vessel's ancient engine.

"You need any help?" she asked. Ray's only response was an embarrassed smile barely camouflaging his frustration.

As far back as she could remember, her parents never took a car to a mechanic. In fact, they hardly ever had service people of any kind come to repair anything. If something was broken, they fixed it themselves. It was a true do-it-yourself household, or households *plural*, that she grew up in. And it must have rubbed off on her more than she had realized. It was probably a combination of that and pure dumb luck which made her seem like a master mechanic at that moment.

"Looks like your problem is the alternator," she said, as they sat together on the floor working on the engine. "And you're probably gonna need a new belt."

Ray's chin quivered, which happened whenever he was about to make a joke. He motioned to the belt that was barely holding up his jeans. "New belt? This one works just fine."

Reilly groaned. "That is such a dad joke."

"Well, I *am* a dad, so..." Ray shrugged, unapologetic about his dorkiness. It was a thin line of defense, but it wasn't untrue. "Speaking of being a dad, my daughter seems to be quite enamored with you."

The second degree of separation compliment flattered her. Reilly was relieved that she'd passed the daughter test. "The feeling is mutual. She's a cool kid."

"She gets that from her mother."

"Judging by your jokes, I'm not surprised."

Ray laughed. "So how did you manage to find yourself in our little town for Christmas?" Ray cleared a strand of Reilly's hair that had fallen into her face, gently tucking it behind her ear.

There went that tingle at the base of her spine again. *Oh, no. I'm in trouble here.* Whatever was happening between them had rapidly graduated from an innocent crush to something that felt much more powerful. So powerful that, while it was thrilling, it was also a little scary. Like a riptide that looked benign but could drag her out to sea in the blink of an eye. The only choices she had was to try to swim against it back to the shore or give in and let it take her.

Choosing to change the subject, Reilly decided to tell him all about her family's Christmas tradition. "Since we were kids, my sister and I always took turns choosing where the family would spend the holidays." The words coming out of her mouth sounded so vanilla and humdrum, but Ray listened with a fixated gaze. He seemed fascinated at being given the opportunity to get a glimpse inside her secret world.

"It gave my sister and me something to look forward to all year. Then, when my parents retired, we kept the tradition going."

"I like that," Ray said with a wistful smile.

He seemed to appreciate being given a glance into Reilly's world. They sat for another moment. Reilly then put down the wrench in her hand and gave the engine a generous spray of WD-40.

"You weren't kidding. You really are good at this stuff." He gestured to the engine.

"Well, we haven't gotten it started yet." Reilly shrugged, tempering expectations. "This alternator is pretty old."

"You're telling me. Everything on this boat is original."

"You wanna give it a shot?" Reilly hoped she had remedied the engine's issue.

Ray went upstairs to the deck, and she heard him put the key in the ignition. The engine clicked and turned over a few times before chitty-chitty-bang-banging to life. Just as she was about to mentally congratulate herself for her stellar mechanical skills, it unceremoniously cut out.

At first, Reilly wasn't exactly sure what had happened. All she knew was that there was a loud POP, like a firecracker, and she was momentarily blinded by a cloud of smoke. She heard Ray's panicked footsteps descend the stairs.

As he skidded to a stop, he stared at her with concern. But seeing that she wasn't injured and that the effects of the explosion were purely cosmetic, he began to laugh.

Reilly didn't need a mirror to know she was completely covered in engine soot. She probably looked like a coal miner who'd just gotten off a twelve-hour shift.

"I think it's safe to say that you need a new alternator," Reilly said, totally deadpan.

This made Ray erupt into another peal of laughter which was too infectious for Reilly not to join in on.

Chapter 7

As Reilly toweled off from the tepid but decently pressured shower, she wiped the condensation off the mirror to check out her reflection. She had successfully managed to wash out the black soot from her hair and face and was looking somewhat back to normal.

Just as she finished putting on a fresh set of clothes and slapping on the most basic bit of make-up, she heard voices coming from up on deck. *More visitors?* She figured this was how her stay on *The Emma* was going to be. But she didn't mind. Despite her fiercely independent spirit, Reilly wasn't a loner. She preferred having people around.

As she stepped up on deck, Reilly was greeted by Emma who was holding two pairs of skis in her hands. "I brought you groceries. I've already put them away," Emma said. "I heard that my dear old dad showed up completely empty-handed this morning. Then he put you to work. Some host." She shook her head before adding, "Boys."

Reilly smiled. "It's fine." She glanced at the skis. "What are you up to?"

"My dad and I are going skiing. We usually try to get out once or twice a week in the winter."

"I didn't know there were any mountains around here."

Emma and Ray shared a look, and Reilly knew she'd stepped into a pile of impending ridicule.

"There aren't any mountains around here, City Girl," said Ray, his chin quivering. "These are *cross-country* skis."

"Right! *Cross-country* skis. Now that I get a proper look at them, I totally see that." Reilly lied. She still had zero idea what the difference was. "I'd love to go some time." Despite not being a winter sports aficionado, she'd give it a shot.

"What size are your feet?" Emma asked.

"Six-and-a-half." Reilly knew the girl was up to something.

"You're in luck. We're the same size. You can use my skis and boots."

Both Reilly and Ray looked at Emma, confused. "What are *you* going to wear?" Ray asked.

"Dad, I totally forgot that I've got to go help with the setting up of the lightwalk today." Emma then turned to Reilly, explaining. "Every Christmas, some of the townsfolk get together and set up a lightwalk through the forest. I've been put in charge of designing it this year," she said proudly.

"I didn't know you had to be there today." Suspicion coated Ray's voice.

Emma gave him a slow, innocent shake of her head. "Working in the arts is like being a doctor, Dad. You're always on call."

He turned to Reilly. "You've never cross-country skied before." He didn't seem upset at the prospect of spending the afternoon with her, but the tone of his voice made it clear that he wanted to get a decent workout without having to babysit a newbie.

"*Of course,* I have!" Reilly teased, laying on the overconfidence. "Sometimes I cross-country ski to work instead of taking an Uber."

Ray grinned. "Okay, City Girl."

At the far end of the dock, near the edge of the woods, Reilly clicked into the ski bindings with the assistance of Emma who steadied her. In front of them was a winding spaghetti strand of a snowy trail leading into an endless forest of trees winter-stripped of all their leaves. Reilly now also wore Emma's gloves, earmuffs, and scarf. She had packed appropriately for the weather, but she hadn't expected to be partaking in any winter Olympic events.

She tried not to appear wobbly as she stood on the skis, but it was akin to riding a bicycle without the training wheels for the first time.

Ray stood on his own skis next to her.

"You ready?"

In place of a verbal response, Reilly lost her balance and toppled onto the ground, dominoing Ray along with herself in the process. As the two lay on the ground, she burst out laughing and began waving her arms back and forth in the freshly fallen, powdery blanket of snow.

"We could just stay here and make snow angels instead."

Ray laughed, as well, as he kissed any possibility of a sufficient afternoon workout goodbye.

As Reilly followed Ray through the sublime forest trail, she very quickly realized that skiing cross-country didn't necessarily mean that the route would be flat, as one might reasonably assume. In fact, the two had been on a murderously relentless slow incline for the best part of twenty minutes, and Reilly's legs were on fire. It was like being trapped on an elliptical machine. Reilly hated elliptical machines.

Numerous times on the journey, she inwardly cursed herself for not keeping her big mouth shut. Regardless, she did try to keep up with Ray to avoid any more embarrassing incidents. After the events of the morning, she didn't want to end up 3-for-3 in the screw-up department.

The slow burn of a climb was all worth it, however, when the two finally and breathlessly came to an opening at the crest of the trail. It was a look out at an astonishing peak over the whole of Mistletoe Lake below. Given how high up they were, Reilly wanted to mention that they'd do well to have proper *downhill* skis in order to get back down to water level, but she didn't want to belabor the issue.

Ray pulled out a Thermos of coffee, poured some into the lid/cup, and handed it to her.

"What, no Irish cream?" Reilly grinned after a warming sip.

"I was tempted to put some in before we left, but you looked pretty wobbly on your skis, so I thought better of it."

Reilly inched closer to the edge and gazed out at the view. Below she could see the boats in the harbor all in a further stage of decorations. From this distance, the vessels looked like toys. It reminded Reilly of Emma's window design in the general store.

"So how did this whole Christmas Harbor Festival start?" She figured it was a pretty basic-making-conversation-type-of-question for two people on a cross-country skiing first date.

Date? Was that what this was? Before she could answer her own question, Reilly caught something passing quickly over Ray's face, like a wispy cloud past a full moon. *Was it somehow too personal of a question?*

"It was my dad, actually. He wanted to do something special for my mom one Christmas. So, on Christmas Eve he stayed up all night decorating our boat with lights and ornaments to surprise her. She loved it so much that they started doing it every year. Pretty soon, everyone on the lake began decorating *their* boats, too, and it became a local tradition." The glint of the memory in Ray's eyes grew as he recounted the story. "After my dad passed, all the locals got together and kept the tradition going in honor of his memory.

"That's so wonderful." Reilly noticed he had a faraway look on his face, staring back into the images in his head.

"Your family really does have a deep connection to the lake."

The glint in Ray's eyes disappeared. "But, not long after, many of the year-rounders moved away, replaced by tourists."

"Seasonals," Reilly called back to their joke. Ray smiled, but she could tell that this was a sore spot for him. As he continued, he surprised her with his openness.

"They continued the festival without knowing how or why it started. It just wasn't the same."

"Why did all the locals move away?" Reilly knew she was stepping into delicate territory. Ray didn't seem to mind, though. Perhaps he appreciated having someone to talk to about it.

"Mistletoe Lake used to be this perfectly kept secret of cottage country. Then some rich guy came along one day, I think he was a movie star or something and bought one of the old cottages. He renovated it to the point where it wasn't a cottage anymore. Instead, it was a mansion on the lake. More people came and did the same thing. Before long, the cost of living got so high here that the locals couldn't afford it anymore. Even the small fishing boats were replaced with mini yachts."

Ray took a sip of coffee. As he fiddled with the cup, Reilly sensed he was embarrassed for having overshared.

"Still, you must be very proud that your dad started such a unique festival."

Ray nodded. A moment passed. The two just listened to the silence of the forest.

"If you wanted to enter the harbor festival this year, you know for the last time and all, I'd be very happy to help."

He gave her a look. It wasn't reproachful, but it was clear this was a topic he'd given a lot of thought to and was torn over. Just when Reilly felt like she'd overstepped, Ray said, "I'd like that," with the earnestness of someone relieved to be getting something off their chest. "But..." he continued, "that offer for the boat could come through any day. I'd hate to tell Em that we're entering the festival and then have to sell before it happens. That would break her heart."

As much as Ray seemed haunted by having to sell his father's boat, Reilly could see that he would prefer to take that heartbreak on himself rather than have any sadness affect his daughter.

Chapter 8

On the way back through the forest, with the swish of their skis performing a duet with the breeze in their ears, Reilly thought about the profoundly different context that the Christmas Harbor Festival represented now.

A few months ago, it was simply just the result of a random internet search that had caught her interest and which she wanted to explore. Now, she'd gotten a glimpse of it through Ray's eyes along with those more granular details of how it was connected to a family's history that most people who visit were oblivious to. Those people just wanted to come see pretty lights and go home again.

Reilly was relieved when they arrived at a clearing in the woods. Just beyond the canopy of snow-dusted evergreens stood a paint-chipped wooden barn where a group of bundled-up locals was unpacking crates of Christmas ornaments.

Amongst the faces, Reilly picked out Emma's. Like a humble but-in-charge foreman on a building site, she was politely giving direction to the group of volunteers, all of whom were easily more than twice her age.

Some of the oversized crystal blue and gold ornaments had already been hung on some of the branches. More volunteers were on ladders stringing constellations of colored lights through the trees.

Seeing Reilly and Ray, Emma smiled and ran over, crunching through the crème brûlée crust of the snow.

"Emma, this is really cool," Reilly encouraged.

"Thanks. I'm really excited for you to see it when it's finished. My vision is to replicate the Christmas Tree Cluster. It's this astronomical constellation formed in the shape of a Christmas Tree."

As Reilly listened, she again marveled at Emma's artistic passion. She wondered if she'd be able to regain her own, or if it was something that had been robbed from her in adulthood.

"I want people to feel as though they are on a guided walk through the stars," Emma continued.

Reilly could only shake her head. "How are you so brilliant?"

"Don't look at me," Ray interjected.

Emma answered the question sincerely, as though it were in no way rhetorical. "I read a lot. Plus, I'm an only child."

She didn't elaborate on how the second part was relevant, but Reilly assumed that her lack of siblings gave her more time to dedicate to accumulating knowledge. *Would I have been smarter without Tara around?*

"Hey, Ray!" came a bellowing voice from inside the barn. Out stepped a Paul Bunyan-looking type of fellow. He had the same neckless broad shoulders and lumberjack gait, but instead of a pirate-like beard, he shaped his facial hair into two large, mutton-chop sideburns which gave him something of an early 70s Elvis Presley look.

As the man took several elephantine steps toward them, he clapped his catcher's mitt-like hands together, which sounded like someone had set off a cherry bomb, and chuckled heartily.

"Ray Mitchell!" He repeated as he vigorously shook Ray's hand.

"Good to see you, Topher." Ray shook his hulking hand.

His name was Topher Bellows, and as far as Reilly could gather, he was the local handyman and jack-of-all-trades. One look at him, and Reilly suspected he'd never set foot outside the boundaries of Mistletoe Lake and never planned to.

"I hear you're selling your dad's boat?" Topher said to Ray, telegraphing that he wasn't one to stay away from town gossip.

Ray pursed his lips and nodded tightly in response. He then glanced at Emma at the mention of the subject.

"Aw, that's a shame," Topher continued, oblivious to the sensitivity of the topic.

Apparently, he was one of those people who was incapable of speaking at a decibel level below a dull shout. *Appropriate that his last name is Bellows.*

"Your dad's boat was the cornerstone of this community! Without *The Emma* in Mistletoe Lake's harbor, this town will never be the same again." Ray's efforts to put on a brave face were negated by the conflict in his eyes, obvious to everyone. Except Topher.

"Speaking of…did you hear the news?" Topher stepped a little closer, obviously excited to impart another tidbit of gossip. His voice, however, didn't get any quieter. "The Mistletoe Lake Harbor is for sale."

Ray gave him a puzzled look. "The...*entire harbor?*"

"Yeah. The municipality is on the verge of bankruptcy. So, they've put the whole harbor on the block."

For such potentially disturbing news, Reilly was surprised at the joy in Topher's voice. Perhaps it was just from the satisfaction of spreading a fresh piece of gossip to new ears.

"I guess they're hoping some private investor will come along and bail them out," Topher reasoned.

Ray shifted his stance, clearly a little on edge. "Who's got that kind of money?" He clearly wasn't looking for an answer, but that didn't stop Topher.

"Not me." He chuckled. "I'm still a million bucks short of having a million bucks!" Then he gleefully clapped his hands together again, setting off another cherry bomb crack that caused everyone to jump.

Chapter 9

Evening fell over the placid lake like a time-lapse shot. Reflections of the fat, pearly stars in the clear night sky shone on the glazed surface of the water as though it were a window into some identical, upside-down, bizarro world below.

On the deck of *The Emma,* underneath the glowing amber hiss of a propane heater and its six-foot circumference of warmth, Reilly, Ray, and Emma sat enjoying a homemade dinner of spaghetti. It was homemade insofar as they'd boiled the pasta, heated the sauce, and added them together. Still, with the freshly baked bread from the local bakery and a glass of pinot noir from the vineyard a couple of towns over, it was the perfect meal.

Ray had politely said goodnight to Reilly earlier. However, Emma wasn't having any of that. She reminded her father that it was Wednesday. And Wednesday was spaghetti night. Emma all but insisted that they all dine together. She didn't need to push too hard, though, as Reilly was happy for the company. It struck her as odd that she was, too. Normally, Reilly would have begun to feel a little claustrophobic at this point. But this was somehow different.

As the three cooked together, Emma stressed the importance of making sure the noodles were *al dente*, while Ray did his very best to convince his daughter, Reilly, too, that the term al dente was coined by a famous Italian chef named *Alberto Dentissimo,* the inventor of spaghetti.

To add context, Ray did his impression of Alberto, complete with an atrocious Italian accent. Reilly surmised that this was a well-worn joke that they trotted out every spaghetti night. Emma gave Reilly permission to ignore her dorky dad, which only added fuel to Ray's fire. He began throwing strands of spaghetti at Emma while doubling down on his bad impression. It had almost resulted in a full-on food fight before being mediated by Reilly.

As Emma spooned another helping onto her plate, she eyed her dad.

Once again, that devious hamster in her head is spinning its wheel.

"Dad, I was doing some research on the structure of business deals."

Ray dabbed the corners of his mouth with his napkin. "I *knew* getting you that unlimited Wi-Fi plan was a mistake." He was being playful, but Reilly could see there was some truth in the statement.

"Knowledge is power, father." Emma bounced one of her eyebrows as though it were on a trampoline.

Reilly giggled as Ray topped up her wine.

"Did you know that you can put these things in business deals called clauses?" Emma continued.

Ray's chin quivered, once again telegraphing that another joke was coming. *He'd be a terrible poker player.*

"Clauses? Are you talking about the Santa kind?"

Reilly and Emma both groaned. "Another thing you should know about my dad," Emma rolled her eyes, "he *loves* his dad jokes."

"Believe me, I'm getting that."

Ray was unapologetic. "Hey, I *am* a dad, so I'm legally allowed to make dad jokes."

Emma shook her head in mock disapproval then steered the conversation back to the matter she carefully wanted to broach. "In a business deal, you can put a *clause* in, and it's like asking for something that you want."

"Where are you going with this, Em?" Ray asked in a wary tone of voice. Reilly didn't doubt he was used to being outfoxed by his daughter.

"You could put a clause in the deal for the boat that the buyer has to take possession *after* Christmas. That way we could still enter it into the harbor festival."

With the bottomless optimism of a young person, Emma was trying to find the best possible solution to their difficult situation. From her still outsider's perspective, though that was rapidly changing with each passing second, Reilly could see that the girl's motivation was out of pure selfless love for her father.

"Well…" Ray hesitated, "I suppose I could ask."

Emma's eyes nearly popped out of her head. She clearly never expected this long-shot to work.

"*You will?*" As she started jumping up and down, Ray tried to temper his daughter's giddiness.

"That doesn't necessarily mean it's happening, Em. I'm just gonna ask. So don't get your hopes up."

Emma's face said it was already too late. Her hopes had skyrocketed. She threw her arms around Ray and squeezed him tightly. "Just for that, I'm gonna do the dishes."

Ray gave her a sideways look. "You always do the dishes on spaghetti night."

"Yeah. But I'm going to do them *extra well* tonight."

As Emma grabbed the tomato sauce-smeared empty plates off the table, she said, "If you guys want dessert, I brought a bag of marshmallows from the store." She then stage-whispered with a wink to Reilly, "They're my dad's favorite."

"What happened to keeping me on a healthy diet?" Ray asked Emma.

She raised one shoulder. "Everybody gets a cheat day, dad. This is yours."

As Emma disappeared into the boat's cabin, Reilly grinned at Ray. "She's quite something."

"She has a lot of her mother in her. But I do see a lot of myself, too. I was exactly the same way with my parents. I suppose it's all payback now."

"How often do you get to see each other?"

"Most holidays. We get at least four big visits a year." It was obvious Ray relished every moment that he could spend with his little girl.

Reilly looked out once more at the lake. It had gotten so dark that the horizon was indiscernible from the sky. The boat creaked as it moved slightly in the raven water.

"I sure do like it here." She still couldn't put her finger on exactly what it was about this place that filled her soul. Maybe it wasn't only one thing, but a collection of the whole. Even so, as she looked at Ray across the table, there was no question that certain aspects were much more significant than others.

"It's rare for someone from the city to like the country so much." The orange glow from the heat lamp danced in his eyes.

Reilly squinted at him. "Are you calling me a City Girl again?"

"No, I swear, I'm not." Ray's voice rose half an octave. "It's just that most people who come to visit try to bring the city with them. But you fit in so well."

"There's something special about a small town. A different kind of frequency than what you find in the city. It's real. And so peaceful."

As if on cue, their tranquil moment was interrupted by…Marky Mark and the Funky Bunch's *Good Vibrations.*

Reilly scrambled to answer her phone. Just as the woman was singing: *sweeeeeeet sensationnnnnnnn,* she hit *Ignore.* Only seconds later, the phone dinged with a text message. She gave Ray an apologetic smile.

"Do you need to respond to that?"
Reilly shook her head and put her phone on silent.

Chapter 10

They moved from the dining table over to the stern of the boat where they sat, wrapped in blankets, with their feet dangling over the edge and their freshly re-filled wine glasses between them.

"You never wanted to live anywhere else?" The warmth of the wine met the comfort of the blanket around her shoulders halfway.

Ray looked out into the darkness, "I left for the city when I was in my twenties." Then his chin-tell betrayed him again as he looked at Reilly. "You know that *one* city where all those people live?"

Reilly laughed. "*The* city. I know it well."

"I liked it. But the day I left my dad told me I'd be back. 'Nothing beats home' he used to say. And he was right." Ray took a sip of wine.

There was that contemplative tone again. It crept into his voice whenever he spoke about his father. As though he was still a little boy.

"But when I got back, the town was almost unrecognizable. There were spring-breakers jet skiing and trendy food trucks in the harbor. We even got a microbrewery here. Before I knew what a microbrewery was, I would've guessed it was a bar for mice." Hearing the words he'd just spoken,

Ray stopped himself. "Wow. That's *another* dad joke. I don't even realize I'm doing it anymore."

"We need to get you a shock collar or something."

Ray's smile dimmed, as though he was suddenly trying to make sense of something. His world? His life? She couldn't tell. He glanced at Reilly with those open-book eyes.

"If I'm being honest, the real reason I'm hesitant to enter the boat into the Christmas Harbor Festival has as much to do with me as it does Emma."

It was evident that the half-truth explanation he'd given her earlier weighed on him, and he needed to come clean.

"In what way?"

"Having to sell the boat is difficult enough. I guess part of me is worried that seeing it in the Harbor Festival will make it that much harder."

"Maybe, but it might also give you some closure."

Ray didn't seem entirely convinced.

She sat with him another moment in silence while the urge to touch him grew stronger. She wanted to feel her hand on his, but she hesitated, allowing her ever-present second-guessing nature to win the moment.

Then a voice from the dock below cut through the quiet.

"Good evening!" If Reilly wasn't so surprised by it, she would have instantly realized that the voice was a familiar one to her.

Edward Louis stood on the dock, smiling up at them, "Hope I'm not interrupting. I was out for an evening stroll and thought I'd come by and say hello."

Thinking that he was speaking to her, Reilly was completely caught off-guard. *How did he know I was here?* Had he been following her?

As this slot machine of questions rolled through her mind, Ray stood up and said to Edward, "You're not interrupting at all. Come on up."

It was only then that Reilly realized Edward wasn't speaking to her but rather Ray. *How did these two know each other?*

Anxiety she couldn't explain erupted in her gut like a slow-moving volcano. Perhaps it was due to the meeting of her two very different worlds.

As Edward made his way onto the boat, his eyes lit up in a pleasant reaction as he noticed Reilly for the first time. "Oh, hello, Reilly!"

Now, it was Ray's turn to be confused. "You two know each other?"

"Edward is one of my clients."

Edward placed a hand on Reilly's shoulder as he proudly told Ray, "Reilly is the very best home stager I've ever worked with. I can't tell you how well I've done in my property investments over the years because of her. In fact," he said, adding a cherry on the cake, "it was Reilly who inspired me to visit Mistletoe Lake."

Ray, still completely lost, glanced at Reilly. "Is that right?"

"I guess you could say that," was all Reilly could manage in response before changing the subject.

"What brings you out this evening, Edward?"

His voice took on a thought-you'd-never-ask tone. "Well, I always take a post-dinner walk. So, I figured I'd come by to have another look at this boat I'm thinking of buying."

Those last four words echoed in Reilly's head as she clung to the slim hope that this boat Edward was referring to just happened to be *another* boat for sale in the same harbor.

As Ray turned to her and explained, "Edward is my potential buyer." That slim hope crumbled and fell like a losing move in Jenga.

Reilly couldn't believe it. It wasn't necessarily a bad thing; it had nothing to do with her. Still, she had that uneasy sensation of being in the middle of something she didn't particularly want to be in the middle of.

"More than potential," Edward corrected Ray. "I'm *very* interested. I'm going to make my decision and let you know shortly." He then ran his finger along the smooth wood paneling in what appeared to be admiration for the decor.

But Reilly knew better. Edward wasn't the kind of guy to appreciate such classic taste. Perhaps he was doing it for show? Or to be polite? Or both.

Ray misconstrued this as an opportunity to talk up the vessel's features.

"That's all-original cherry wood. My dad took exquisite care of this boat. It was his pride and joy."

Edward nodded his approval. "Clearly."

"I've been having a little trouble with the engine's alternator, but I'll have it fixed before the sale goes through," Ray said. Then, perhaps in an effort not to appear overly desperate, added, "*If* you decide to buy it, that is."

Edward smiled. It was the practiced gesture of a successful businessman who was used to being in control. "I'm sure it will all be fine. And I promise to let you know very soon. I'm just waiting to hear back from my accountant on a few things." He gave the boat another 180° gander. "I do so like this vessel. It's perfect for what I'm looking for."

Reilly couldn't help but be suspicious. *What does Edward want with this boat?* In all the time that she'd known him, granted only a year and change, he'd never expressed any nautical aspirations. Then again, what did she know? Anything was possible with a guy like Edward.

With a lull in the conversation, Ray seemed apprehensive, like a diver on the edge of a cliff deciding whether to jump or not. Finally, he took the plunge.

"Edward, if you *do* decide to buy the boat, would you possibly be open to taking possession *after* Christmas?"

Edward gave him a puzzled look, but Ray pressed on. "You see, my daughter has this dream about entering the Harbor Festival one last time." A cloud of uncertainty passed over Edward's face.

"Oh…" Edward began awkwardly, "I was planning on having my family visit over Christmas." He then paused. Underneath that slick exterior, Reilly believed he had a good heart. "But I understand your daughter's desire to have a last

Christmas here." He mulled it over, clearly looking for a compromise.

"Would you be willing to have me, my sister, and her kids join you for the Christmas Harbor celebrations if the deal goes through?"

Relief flushed on Ray's face. "Absolutely. Your whole family is welcome no matter what you decide."

With the satisfaction of another successful negotiation, Edward smiled. "Very well then. I'll call you tomorrow."

The two shook hands with one firm press, and Edward turned to go. Before he stepped down onto the dock, he looked back at Reilly. "Let's have that lunch." Then he was gone, his loafers clicking away along the creaky wooden dock until the darkness enveloped him.

Alone again, Reilly and Ray shared a look. Ray's face betrayed his confusion. "So bizarre that you two know each other. What a coincidence."

Reilly smiled tightly. "Yeah. Crazy."

Ray took a deep breath. "I hope I'm doing the right thing by delaying the sale until after Christmas."

"Emma will be ecstatic," Reilly said, knowing that was the most important thing for him.

"And Edward seems like a nice guy. I mean, he's not a *local*, but at least he wants the boat for his family. I have nothing against the seasonals. But for years, I've seen people swoop in and buy up so much of the town, pushing out people who call it home. It just doesn't seem fair." Ray then looked at Reilly "Edward is a good guy, right?"

On the spot, she stammered, "Yeah," then added, "I mean, I don't know him *really* well. But…overall, yes." And she truly meant that. *Still, why am I feeling so awkward?*

Ray looked up at the framed hanging on the wall. "*The Emma* is my last true memory of my father. I'd hate to have someone come along and completely gut it. Turn it into something unrecognizable. I'm glad Edward wants to use the boat for his family. Having people here who are going to enjoy it like we did for so many years is a bit of a silver lining to selling."

Ray paused, seeming to momentarily have convinced himself that he was doing the right thing. Emerging from what had to be a whirlwind of thoughts and emotions, he looked again at Reilly. "I guess I better go tell my daughter the good news."

As Ray went inside the boat's cabin, Reilly pulled the blanket she held more tightly around her shoulders. That uneasy feeling in her gut didn't want to go away.

Emma's yelp of delight echoed across the slushy lake.

Moments later, Ray emerged from the cabin, the joy at making his daughter's night etched into his face. "She's happy."

Reilly chuckled. "No, really? I couldn't tell at all."

He took another few steps until he was closer to her than he'd even been in the brief amount of time they'd known each other. "I'm sorry to have dumped all of this stuff onto you. You're just trying to enjoy your Christmas vacation."

"Not a problem. I'm happy to be a sounding board. Besides I've got an amazing place to stay and an incredible dinner out of it tonight to boot."

The corners of Ray's mouth were tugged into that mischievous grin once again. "We forgot about dessert."

Only then did Reilly realize he was holding something behind his back. It was the jumbo bag of marshmallows.

"Let's go."

Chapter 11

Bundled up in scrounged winter jackets and a shared blanket, huddling in front of a glowing wood teepee fire on the lakeshore, Reilly and Ray sat on a sideways beached log.

Aware that their legs were touching through the cloth of clothing, neither moved. The non-verbalized reason was that it was a cold winter night, but they both knew it was something more, that they'd both subconsciously agreed to give up resisting this gravitational pull between them.

"It must have been quite something to grow up here." Reilly carefully rotated her marshmallow impaled on the stick like a rotisserie to ensure equal crispiness on all sides. "I'm kinda jealous." Adding to the aura, above them, the stars shone over Mistletoe Lake as though they were in their own planetarium.

The two had been sitting on the frozen beach, gazing through the flames of the fire Ray had built engaging in getting to know you talk. Huddled together, staring through the frolicking flames at the shifting icy lake in front of them, a person couldn't help but open up.

Ray held his roasting stick over the fire masterfully, clearly having had much more practice than Reilly. "Was there ever a place in your childhood that you felt at home?"

He turned his gaze slowly toward her and the topic of conversation away from himself.

The question instantly sparked a memory within Reilly, simultaneously with a firecracker pop in the fire. "One place. When I was about eight years old. 9 Deanewood Crescent."

Through the wormhole of her mind, Reilly was transported back to that beloved suburban home. "It was this little house, with a crooked picket fence, white, of course, and a crabapple tree in the front yard that my sister and I used to climb. The house wasn't anything overly special to look at, but it was so cozy. I hoped we'd stay there forever."

"*Deanewood.* Sounds like something out of *Leave it to Beaver.*" Ray stuck a fresh marshmallow onto Reilly's twig, replacing the one that had caught fire and had fallen to its demise in the white-hot coals.

"It kinda was. I'll never forget the day our parents sat us down and told us the house had been sold, and we'd be moving again. Broke my heart." Reilly left out the detail of the day being *Christmas Day.* Out of context, it would have sounded an overly cruel and unusual moment to break that kind of news to your children.

"Nothing beats home." Ray re-iterated as Reilly sat momentarily in the memory.

"The year we spent at that house it was my turn to pick our Christmas holiday destination. And I chose to stay home. A *staycation*, long before anybody knew what that was. It was one of my favorite Christmases ever."

"What's your middle name?" he asked.

Reilly couldn't hide the puzzlement on her face at the out-of-nowhere question. "Why?"

"I wanna know what your soap opera name is—your middle name plus the place you grew up." Ray grinned.

"Do we know each other well enough for that?" Reilly asked, evading. She never liked her middle name, and thus did her best to conceal it at every possible opportunity.

"C'mon. It can't be any worse than City Girl," Ray said. "I'll tell you mine if you tell me yours."

Reilly gave him a sideways glance. *That old chestnut.* She took a breath. Their evening was going so well. This could make it or break it. He could find it endearing or as hideously off-putting as she did. It was a toss-up.

"Mildred," Reilly finally said, the word coming out in a sigh of embarrassment.

Ray paused a moment, his eyes searching her face to make sure she was serious. Her grave look said it all. A giggle erupted from him. Perhaps he found it both endearing *and* hideous at the same time.

"I was named after my great aunt," Reilly said with playful defensiveness.

Ray's giggle graduated into a full-on laugh. "*Mildred Deanewood.* That is some soap opera name."

Reilly joined in the laughter. Part of her, though, registered his touch on her. It was heavy and sent a jolt of electricity through her whole body.

"Okay, tell me yours." A deal was a deal.

Suddenly stoic, Ray considered for a moment. "No. It's too embarrassing."

"Cheater!" Reilly shrieked, playfully pushing him.

After carefully placing the new log on top of the crispy foundation of the ones that went before it, Ray sat back down next to Reilly, allowing his arm to slide around the small of her back. It was a smooth move but done by a guy who was clearly out of practice at smooth moves, which made it all the more charming to Reilly.

"Can I ask you a personal question?"

"*Another* personal question? Is this one as embarrassing as the last?" Reilly asked, half joking.

He shook his head. "Not at all. I don't think so, anyway."

She nodded. She was unsure of what was coming, however, on the heels of the middle name debacle, she was ready for anything.

"How is it that someone like you is single?"

"How do you know I'm single?" Reilly asked, flirtatiously putting Ray on his heels.

"I-I-I suppose I don't," he stammered, "I just figured that since you're here at the holidays by yourself—"

"Emma told you; didn't she?" Reilly interrupted, not wanting to let him squirm too much.

"Yes." He'd been caught. "But to be fair, she held out as long as she could. It was only when I threatened to cancel the Netflix account that she sang like a canary."

"Ruthless." Reilly grinned. She was happy that Emma seemed to be on board with this obvious attraction between her and Ray. It said a lot about a kid who wanted to see her parents happy despite their break-up. It also said a lot about Ray as a dad.

"Is it the same old story of being married to your work?" He asked.

"Not really. My sister is more the workaholic." She wanted to let him in, but she didn't want to overshare. "I was engaged once."

"What happened?"

Reilly considered for a moment. It was something she'd given an exhaustive amount of thought to over the past year. Still, it was difficult to reduce into a somewhat succinct answer.

"Everyone used to say how perfect we were for each other." A smattering of images of Greg montaged in her head like Polaroids stuck on a fridge—her thirtieth birthday weekend, that selfie they took on their first date riding the Ferris wheel at Navy Pier, that aborted skydiving afternoon outing where they both chickened out at the last minute.

"And I felt the same. We had the perfect house. The perfect car. The perfect life." That fresh log, now fully engulfed in flames, timbered over in the fire, sending a scattering of sparks to sizzle and be snuffed out on the snowy surrounding ground. "Then...one morning I woke up, and I realized that what *looked* perfect wasn't perfect at all. I just couldn't do it anymore."

More images flashed into Reilly's head—that morning around the kitchen island in their old apartment—the one she presumed Greg still lived in—it was originally his, after all. The two of them crying, yet still having to deal with mundane details like work. Reilly at the packing supply store in a zombified daze buying boxes and rolls of tape, trying to do the mental math of how many she'd need for all her worldly belongings. "It was a tough break-up, but in the end, it was much better for both of us."

Ray didn't push for more details. And she'd taken him as far down the river of her past heartbreak that she could.

"I know all about tough break-ups. Emma's mom and I are on good terms, thankfully. But we got to a point where we realized that we were better as friends than a married couple."

Several quiet moments passed. Behind them, the night wind crawled through the trees in the distance.

"That's another difficult thing about selling the boat," Ray continued, "Emma has already had to go through the break-up of me and her mother. My biggest fear is letting her down again. I don't know what I would do if I lost her. She's everything to me."

Reilly read the genuine fear in his eyes. "You won't lose her." She didn't know how she could possibly know that. Yet, she just knew.

"She's so talented. And smart. She's applied to this private art school in New Hampshire—Grafton Arts Academy. It's expensive, but if she gets in, at least I can use some of the money from the boat's sale for her tuition."

"You're a good dad," Reilly said as she put her hand on top of Ray's. She hadn't planned on doing that; it just happened.

He turned his hand over, so their palms were touching and gave the slightest squeeze. "In spite of my dad jokes?"

"Amazingly so, yes."

They moved even closer to each other, which was quite close since they had started out practically on top of each other.

"Do you know why it's called Mistletoe Lake?" Ray asked, while unblinkingly holding eye contact with her.

Reilly shook her head. The question had never occurred to her.

"Because mistletoe grows wild all around the woods here. The legend goes that the tradition of kissing under the mistletoe was started right here in this very town. We're quite proud of that."

"I can tell. Based on all the mistletoe trinkets on display in the general store alone." Reilly tried to appear nonchalant despite the growing intensity of the moment.

"Those things keep the lights on in that place." Ray replied, "Tourists eat them up like candy."

"You mean seasonals, right?" It had been a very long time since Reilly was in a romantic situation like this.

"I was thinking of getting one of those shirts that say, *Kiss me I went to Mistletoe Lake,*" Reilly said, aware of the double entendre and hoping it wasn't too obvious.

Ray smirked. "Sounds like something that's right up your alley. It would go perfectly with your Christmas ornament earrings."

Reilly blushed. "What Christmas ornament earrings?"

"Those red heart ornament earrings you were wearing when you first came into the store."

"You saw those?"

"First thing I noticed about you. Well, one of the first, anyway."

"Busted," Reilly conceded.

"I thought they were adorable."

"You do know that the mistletoe tradition comes from Greek mythology, right?" Reilly said, hoping not to burst Mistletoe Lake's fantasy bubble.

"Yeah. Saturnalia, the ancient Greek version of Christmas."

Reilly was impressed. "Check out the big brain on Ray."

He shrugged. "I just knew that bachelor of arts in humanities would come in handy one day." Reilly burst out laughing. "The way I see it if the town wants to take responsibility for people kissing at Christmas, what's the harm?" He doubled down on the double entendre.

They locked eyes. This was the moment that they were either going to go for it or not. Reilly bit her bottom lip.

"So…there must be some mistletoe nearby right now, don't you think?"

He moved his face closer to hers. "Absolutely. We're surrounded by it."

She moved her face closer to his. Their noses were almost touching. "Well, we shouldn't break tradition, should we?" A sultry rasp crept into her voice.

"Definitely not." Ray's gaze moved down her face to her lips. "Without traditions, we'd be left with only anarchy."

The moment was there for the taking, and Reilly took it, pulling Ray in for a kiss. As their lips met, a swoon of intoxication rose in her gut.

Ray slid his hand inside her jacket and around her waist, pulling her closer. She could feel the cool of his skin through the thin cotton layer of her t-shirt. The two drank each other in. The steady thrum of his heartbeat had her guessing if this was his first bit of romance after a long hiatus, much like her.

When they finally came apart, their gazes continued to hold. Silently, they acknowledged a line had been crossed. There wasn't any going back from here.

Chapter 12

The following day, Reilly held Ray's hand as they slowly walked through the corridor of light. It was otherworldly, a shimmering canopy of colors that transported them to an extra-terrestrial-esque dimension. It didn't hurt that both she and Ray were still intoxicated by the buzzy high that comes along with new love.

Was it actually love? Perhaps that was premature. Infatuation, maybe? Enchantment? Passion? Lust? Or a pot-luck combination thereof? The feeling could make even the most mundane of experiences fun. However, in an environment such as this one, it was a perfect storm of knee-watering romance.

As Reilly and Ray floated through the Christmas light-walk—a sparkling corridor of trees illuminated through the dark, late afternoon woods, the two found themselves momentarily alone in an alcove of silver light.

Reilly pulled Ray's hand until it was around her waist and put her lips on his, stealing a kiss, a momentary fix. Until they heard the crunching of other footsteps behind them, pushing them to continue through the exhibit.

Reilly didn't truly recognize herself. It had been so long since this character in the kaleidoscope of different sides of her persona had shown its face. She wasn't exactly the jump-your-bones-in-an-elevator, passionate make-out kind of person. But since she and Ray had kissed, her head had been spinning with love drunkenness.

It was the kind of thing that wasn't sustainable, of course. You couldn't constantly live in a pink bubble of lovey-dovey bliss where everything was a heady romance novel dream sequence. Sooner or later, you'd have to settle back down to earth, where people wore their mouthguards to bed, taxes had to be paid, and garbage taken out.

Still, there's just nothing like this feeling.

As they exited the other side of the lightwalk, they were met by a smiling Emma. Her joy was so radiant that she might as well have been one of the lights in the exhibit.

Seeing Emma, Reilly instinctively let go of Ray's hand. She didn't know exactly how much Ray wanted to tell his daughter about what was happening between them and decided to leave that ball in his court.

However, Reilly saw the kid's eagle-eye catch the briefest of glimpses, a split second before they disentangled their fingers. Nothing got by that kid. Reilly felt a tinge of embarrassment at being caught, almost as though, once again, they were the kids and Emma was the parent but was put at ease after reading the happiness on Emma's face. This was what she wanted. For her dad to be happy.

"It's stunning, Emma. Truly stunning. I felt as though I was stepping into a different world."

"That means a lot, coming from you." Emma beamed.

The lightwalk had been a perfect metaphor for Reilly's experience over these last few days. She had stepped into a different world, momentarily leaving her old one behind. She knew it was bound to catch up. It had already started to. But she was content to enjoy this next experience for as long as it lasted.

Hopefully, forever, she heard a small optimistic voice in her head say. That internal voice was much quieter and more polite than the trumpeting tone of her critical self.

"It's incredible, honey," Ray said, making Reilly wonder what that profound experience of parenthood must be like. To watch this little girl who, at one time, wasn't able to feed herself or walk on her own, growing up and becoming independent. It had to be both exhilarating and heartbreaking at the same time.

Up to this point, motherhood was an undiscovered country for Reilly. She wasn't sure if it was in the cards for her to have that experience or not. While she was with Greg, it was an unspoken presumption that they were going to go there. Until they didn't.

"Thanks, Dad. I really hope I get into Grafton Academy."

"So do I."

Reilly could see his determination to do whatever it took to make that happen. That was the selflessness of parenthood.

Amongst the milling crowd at the lightwalk's exit, Emma called to someone Reilly recognized. "Hi, Grandma!"

The older woman's face lit up as Emma ran to her with open arms. "There's my talented granddaughter!"

A tingle of embarrassment hit Reilly as Emma brought the woman over. When they had met before back at the B&B, Reilly had no context for who she was. Now, in the lifetime since that first encounter had occurred, Reilly felt as though she'd taken a crash course in the family.

"Grandma, this is my new friend, Reilly."

"We met the other day." Reilly extended her hand, perhaps a tad overzealously.

Emmaline smiled politely, and they shook. "I understand you found a place to stay."

Reilly couldn't tell if it was her own paranoia or if there was a curiosity in Emmaline that bordered on mild suspicion. If it was the latter, Reilly wouldn't have blamed her. After all, in Emmaline's eyes, a couple of days ago, Reilly was just some tourist out of luck for a hotel room. Now, she was staying on her son's boat—*her boat?*—having befriended her granddaughter.

"Ray was kind enough to take pity on me and let me stay on the boat." Reilly heard the words coming out of her mouth, and they sounded even more hollow. *The boat? You mean the one that her deceased husband built with his own hands?* Reilly mentally scolded herself.

A pause passed in the conversation that felt long enough to make a U-turn in an aircraft carrier. In an effort to fill that yawning void, Reilly quickly added with a smile to Emmaline, "I hear that the boat is named after you. You must be so proud."

Once again, a tidal wave of mortification washed over Reilly.

I hear that you're named after that boat that your son is now forced to sell due to financial hardships.

Reilly felt like a prize idiot. And not just any prize idiot, but an idiot who won the gold medal at the Global Idiot Olympics.

Emmaline smiled politely again at Reilly. "Yes, that's me."

She couldn't detect any judgment in Emmaline's voice, which almost made it worse. She simply gave Reilly a pleasant, nod before shifting her gaze toward Ray.

"How's the sale progressing?" Unlike her son, Emmaline's expression betrayed nothing of what was going on underneath.

Ray's face was a knot of confliction. "It's…progressing."

"Well, keep me posted." Emmaline turned her kind, if not cagey, eyes back toward Reilly. "It was very nice to meet you."

Ray had been uncharacteristically quiet in their walk home, and that had gotten into Reilly's head. It wasn't as though she'd committed a capital offense or anything with Emmaline. She'd simply mentioned the boat, and while that might be a delicate subject within the family, still, it wasn't as though she'd *sunk* the vessel or anything. Still, she liked the guy and knew that these early moments in a budding relationship were delicate. Whether she'd planned this or not, she was invested now.

As the three arrived at the slip of *The Emma,* Ray and Emma stopped to say their goodnights. Emma, possessing a discretion beyond her years, hung back a few feet, pretending to be looking at something below the surface of the water. In actuality, she was most likely giving her dad a private moment with his new girlfriend. *Girlfriend? Surely, it's way too early for labels.*

Reilly's eyes searched Ray's face, but there was no trace of anything off. His eyes were soft.

"I'm sorry about mentioning the boat to your mother. I wasn't thinking."

Ray shook his head slowly. "It's fine. Really. Having to sell the boat has been tough on the family. We're all dealing with it in our own different ways."

"So…we start decorating the boat tomorrow?" Emma said, knowing her cue to approach like a seasoned stage actor.

"You bet. I can't wait," Reilly said.

"We'll be here bright and early in the morning." Emma gave Reilly a hug goodnight, and she and her dad walked away along the dock.

As she made her way up the gangplank and onto the boat, Reilly could hear Emma and Ray talking as their steps were receding away from her.

Obviously thinking she was out of earshot, Emma asked, "So, what do you think of Reilly? She's super cool, right?"

As they kept getting farther away, Reilly had to strain to hear Ray's mumbled response. "Yeah, she's definitely…interesting." A giddy smile played on Reilly's face as she stepped inside the boat's cabin.

As she poured the final half glass of wine from the previous night's bottle into a glass, Reilly's mind swirled with thoughts of Ray, and the butterflies did cartwheels in her stomach.

She was happy to be able to enjoy this silent moment with just the view and a sip of pinot noir as her company. However, her solitude was interrupted by...*Marky Mark and the Funky Bunch*.

Reilly reluctantly fished her phone out of her pocket and answered.

"Finally! I've been calling you and calling you! Where have you been?" said her slightly petulant sister. Tara hated not getting what she wanted. The trait made her an excellent businesswoman.

"I've just been out...enjoying the town," Reilly said, in a kinda, sorta lie of omission.

"You'll never guess who I spoke to yesterday," Tara barreled through excitedly.

"Edward."

"Yes! How did you know that?"

Reilly didn't want to get into it, but she knew she didn't have much of a choice. "I could just tell by the shrill excitement in your voice."

"He told me he's planning on buying a boat that's for sale on Mistletoe Lake!" Tara's glee spilled through the phone.

Reilly took a substantial sip of her wine and shifted uncomfortably. She knew all too well which boat that was. She was *sitting* in it.

"And he's working on some other stuff, too. I tried to get it out of him, but he wouldn't tell me," Tara continued.

Reilly wasn't entirely convinced that was the whole truth as it wasn't Tara's style to take no for an answer. But Reilly didn't press it. She didn't want to know any more anyway.

"I've been trying to change my flight, but it looks like it's too crazy with Christmas."

As Reilly listened to Tara, she could hear the manic clicking of her mouse.

"So, I told Edward that you'd meet with him before I got there."

Reilly nearly choked on the final sip of wine in her glass. "You did? Why?" She couldn't stand it when her sister's control-freak ways bled over into her own life.

"Because I've got a brilliant idea of how to expand our business," Tara said, with the intonation of an overcaffeinated morning drive radio host.

Her sister had just planted her squarely in the middle of an awkward position. Reilly did her best to diffuse Tara's opportunistic mood. "Tar, I'm sure Edward just wants to buy the boat so he can have somewhere to spend Christmas with his family. There's no business opportunity here."

"There's *always* a business opportunity *everywhere*," Tara calmly replied, before jumping back onto the galloping steed of her ambition. "If we can get the contract to stage and redesign Edward's boat, it will open us up to a whole slew of new opportunities, boats, RVs, glamping—"

Like being in a batting cage where all the balls were pitched to you at once, Reilly scrambled to process the onslaught of information that Tara was force-feeding her.

"—*glamping?*"

Tara had her response coiled and ready like a cobra. "It's a billion-dollar industry, Reilly. I'm telling you the possibilities are endless."

Reilly had learned enough about business in the last year-and-change to know that one should be wary anytime someone uses the term *I'm telling you*. Even if that person was her sister. It was in the same category as the understanding that anyone who says *I hear ya* is not actually listening.

"I'm not staging anyone's boat." Reilly pumped the brakes on this possible nightmare scenario. "It's Christmas. Can't we just give business a rest for the moment?"

"No, we can't, actually, looking at the numbers," Tara scolded. "And besides, I thought you said you were going to look out for business opportunities while you were there?"

"No, *you* said I should look out for business opportunities." The walls steadily closed in. "Besides, Edward's not going to need our services. If he buys the boat, he's probably not going to do anything to change it."

At this, Tara scoffed so loudly, Reilly could almost hear spittle hit the receiver on the other end of the phone. "Oh, please. *Edward Louis?*"

Reilly's mind flashed back to Edward's insistence on stuccoing over the beautiful mahogany hardwood. She shuddered at the thought.

"You wanna bet?" Tara dared her sister.

But that was a bet Reilly wasn't willing to take. Not by a mile.

Chapter 13

Ray and Emma arrived at the boat bright and early the next morning armed with coffee and breakfast wraps from the cafe in town. They had a lot to do to get the boat in shape for the harbor festival and needed to get a jump on the day.

With it being a Saturday, and evidenced by his still sleepy, puffy eyes, Reilly surmised that Ray had most likely been untimely dragged from his bed by an overly excited Emma. Nonetheless, he rallied with a brave face until the caffeine could hit his bloodstream.

The first order of business was to sketch out a schematic diagram and make a master list of items needed. Reilly was very impressed with Emma's preparation. She'd brought graph-paper notebooks, sharpened pencils, and a spreadsheet on her laptop with a very detailed head start on a shopping list. The kid had done her homework.

As Ray worked on the second half of his extra-large coffee, Reilly and Emma came up with a mutual artistic vision for the boat. Once they were on the same page, it was time to go source out supplies. Emma had mapped out the most time-efficient route for all the stores they needed to hit. The three piled into Ray's late-model pickup truck and hit the road.

First stop was the large department store a few towns over. Reilly and Emma descended on the store like a couple of Navy SEALs on a search and rescue mission. They combed every aisle, checking off various items on their master list—sets of hanging lights, wreaths, lengths of garland, and every other item of Christmas decorative paraphernalia imaginable. Ray, relegated to pushing the shopping cart, did his very best to keep up.

Next up, the gang headed to the nursery on the far end of the lake. Instead of a chopped-down Christmas tree, Reilly decided to use a potted evergreen instead. Along with liking the look of the tree, it avoided the unfortunate tradition of cutting down a perfectly good tree in order to decorate it for a few months before unceremoniously throwing it out in January. In keeping with the environmental mindset that was frequent amongst those of her generation, Emma loved the idea. Ray did, as well, until he was tasked with the job of trying to get the dead weight of a six-foot potted tree into the truck.

It took the use of a forklift to get the evergreen into the back of the pick-up. The Herculean effort was worth it, however, even for just the askew looks they got driving around the countryside with a large tree standing tall in the cargo bed.

The penultimate stop on the agenda was at an arts and crafts store in a strip mall off the freeway. There, Reilly and Emma divided and conquered, hunting for paint and brushes, glue, ribbon, staples, and other manner of craft supplies.

The two moved through the store with such economy of time, it was as though they were on one of those shopping spree game shows where contestants only had a certain amount of time to fill their carts. In an attempt to stay out of the way, Ray, unfortunately picked the wrong loose shelf to lean on and found himself nearly drowned in a tsunami of colored yarn. Despite the store manager being acutely unimpressed, the event was a source of great amusement for the girls. Reilly laughed so hard, she actually snorted—an experience she hadn't had since grade school.

By the end of the following day, as the sun was sinking down the lake's horizon like a melting orange popsicle, and a celebratory bottle of local plonk was being uncapped, *The Emma* had been transformed into a vessel of floating Christmas joy with a lot of elbow grease and love. Finishing touches, of course, were still to be applied, but the boat had caught up to, and in many cases *surpassed,* the decorative states of the other boats in the harbor.

"Well, whaddaya think?" Reilly asked Ray after clinking wine glasses with him along with Emma's mug of eggnog.

"I think the other boats in the festival have no idea what they're in for," Ray said proudly. "You and Em have completely raised the bar."

"Don't sell yourself short," Reilly protested.

He raised his hands modestly. "Hey, I'm just the chauffeur, gofer, pusher of shopping carts, and lifter of heavy things. You two are the artistic brains behind the operation."

"Well, we couldn't have done it without you." Emma kissed her dad on the cheek and went back inside for another mugful of eggnog.

Reilly noticed a wistful look make its way across Ray's face.

"What is it?"

"Nothing, just…seeing the boat like this brings back a lot of memories."

Reilly gave his hand a squeeze. It seemed like forever since they'd touched one another.

Emma reappeared onto the deck. "One thing we haven't discussed is what we're going to do for the event."

Reilly looked at her quizzically. *Event?*

Ray sighed. "I totally forgot about that. Topher sent me a message. Apparently, our night is Christmas Eve. No pressure."

Reilly struggled to catch up. "What *event?*"

"The final component of the competition is that each boat has to host a social event one evening," Ray explained.

"So…we've got to plan and host a party, as well? Nobody thought to mention that to me before now?" Reilly's tone was only 75% playful. It was a pretty significant error of omission. Emma and Ray shared a don't-look-at-me look.

Then Ray said, with that casual smirk, "We figured we ought to ease you into it, instead of hitting you with everything at once."

She shook her head with a smile. "Worst Airbnb ever."

"Just wait." Ray doubled down on the sarcasm. "Next we're going to have you scrubbing barnacles off the hull."

"I think throwing a party will be the easy part," Emma said, presumably picking up on the flirtation happening right in front of her. "All we have to do is come up with a theme."

"Well, you know the seasonals will be going all out, flying in chefs to cater and bands to perform." A note of disdain coated Ray's voice. "One year the Dykstras hired *Hootie and The Blowfish* to perform."

Emma crinkled her brow. "What's Hootie and the Blowfish?"

"It's a band from before you were born." Ray looked at Reilly. "Probably you, too."

"Not quite. But thanks." Reilly smiled. She'd seen the band perform back in college.

"Why don't we make our theme something that Mistletoe Lake is all about?" she asked.

"What did you have in mind?"

She'd caught Ray's interest. "Well, what does Mistletoe represent?"

"Kissing. *Love.*" Emma teased.

Reilly tried to suppress the blush that was working its way to the surface of her skin. *Had Emma seen them kissing?*

"Yeah. And *heart*," Reilly continued, in a white-knuckled attempt to sound casual. "So, let's make our party's theme exactly that—the heart of Christmas."

Emma instantly seized upon the idea with excitement. "I love it! Where's the notebook? I've got the perfect idea."

As Emma went to pick up the now dog-eared notebook filled with their sketches and ideas, Ray asked, "Is there anything extra that I need to do for this party?"

Both Reilly and Emma shook their heads, graciously letting him off the hook. Then Emma said, "Well…perhaps other than finding something decent to wear."

Over the past few days, Ray had been cycling through the same three flannel shirts, which were very similar to each other, and two pairs of jeans, which were even more similar.

Ray took playful exception to this as he looked down at his attire. "What's wrong with this?"

Emma burst out laughing. Reilly was close on her heels.

"It's not exactly evening attire. I can take you out shopping for an outfit if you like," Reilly offered.

Ray sighed. "I hate clothes shopping."

"Clearly." Emma's response elicited another round of laughter.

Later that night, as Reilly lay in bed, with the warm blankets tucked up under her chin, and the window open just the tiniest sliver to let the fresh, cold winter air in, she was overcome with excitement. It had happened to her all her life at Christmas. She had an anomalous sensation that this year's Christmas was going to be a very significant one in her life.

She couldn't wait for her sister to arrive so they could all celebrate together. Any worries she'd had about Edward and potential complications were totally drowned out by her sheer joy in the moments ahead. Ray and Emma had already made this Christmas so special for Reilly, she wanted to make sure to do the same for them. It was at that moment that she heard a faint noise come in through the open window from across the lake.

Peering out, Reilly saw a boat in the distance, a toy-sized vessel way out in the middle of the lake, lights shimmering in the darkness. An idea crystallized in Reilly's mind. With bare feet padding across the cold floor, she went to the engine room and looked in at the dormant motor. With her phone, she snapped a photograph, the flash from her phone momentarily illuminating the room like a lightning strike. She then ran back to her bed, grabbing her laptop as she went. Once again snuggled up in the blankets, Reilly opened her computer and typed in a search, the silvery-blue screen shining back on her face.

Chapter 14

The following morning, the nickel-grey sky hung low. An overnight dusting of snow had left its remnants on the tree branches and crevices in the road. Few people were milling about as Reilly made her way along Main Street with a spring in her step.

Her heart ornament earrings swung with every stride she made. Knowing she was going to see Ray, she'd put them on, mostly as an inside joke between them. It also didn't hurt that he'd said he found them adorable.

Up ahead, the town Christmas tree stood in all its glory, the hanging, colored lights on the streetlamps drawing her eyes to it, like the gold chain of a necklace culminating in a diamond pendant.

Reilly saw someone tending to the tree. As she approached, she recognized Emmaline and hesitated. Had they not seen each other, Reilly most likely would have avoided any interaction. But it was too late for that now. She still couldn't put a finger on why she felt uncomfortable around Emmaline. The woman had been nothing but polite to her. Perhaps it had something to with Reilly putting her foot in her mouth the last time they'd met.

"Hello again." Reilly waved and approached Emmaline, who was sweeping up the cones around the base of the tree.

The silver-haired woman smiled warmly. "How is your stay going out on the water?"

"It's lovely. Such a beautiful town, this is." Reilly spoke from the heart.

"It is indeed. We all have to do our part. This year I was assigned caretaker of the communal Christmas Tree." Reilly looked up at the glorious tree. "This tree is about a hundred years old," Emmaline continued. "It was here long before any of us were, and it will hopefully still be here long after we're gone." She continued to sweep.

Reilly lingered a moment. Finally, she said, "Listen, Emmaline, I'm sorry that I was so blasé about bringing up the boat to you the other day. I know the decision to sell it has been difficult for you and your family."

Emmaline stopped sweeping. She rested her hands on top of the broom handle and looked at Reilly for a lingering moment. Her eyes were kind. "Don't be silly." Her words put Reilly at ease. "Having to sell the boat is sad, but I think the person who is taking it the worst is Ray. Even more so than Emma."

"Why do you think that is?" Reilly asked.

Staring off into the distance, Emmaline sighed. "We've all watched our beloved town change over the years. Ray blames the seasonal vacationers for driving up all the prices and causing many of the locals to have to move away." Reilly saw a flash of sadness cross over Emmaline's face.

"He watched his own father nearly go broke trying to stay here." She picked up a fallen ornament and carefully placed it back on the Christmas tree branch. "I suppose, in a way, Ray isn't wrong. But you can't blame the world for changing. And those changes haven't been all bad. Without the vacationers, we would've had to close the B&B long ago. And many of the shops and restaurants in town wouldn't have been able to survive."

Emmaline then looked back to Reilly and smiled. "I'm happy that Ray has decided to enter the boat into the harbor festival one last time. We haven't participated in that in years." Her smile lingered. "If I were a gambling woman, I'd bet his decision has a lot to do with you."

The comment knocked Reilly back on her heels. She reddened. "Me? I think all the credit should go to Emma."

Emmaline shrugged. There was still a twinkle in her eyes. "That may be so, but I haven't seen my son so happy in a long time, and I daresay it's because of you."

Her cheeks hot, Reilly appreciated Emmaline's unspoken blessing.

Chapter 15

In an old-fashioned town such as Mistletoe Lake, it would be difficult to imagine what a vintage clothing store could do to differentiate itself from all the other shops in town, but Vinnie's Vintage Shoppe on Main Street did its best, starting with the gingham dresses and tweed suits hanging in the window.

As she approached, Reilly saw Ray standing outside waiting for her. Anyone else, particularly anyone back home, would have been standing, head down, mindlessly thumbing through their phone. But not Ray. He just stood there, ever present in the moment.

When his gaze found Reilly as she walked toward him, he broke out into a smile that warmed her from a dozen feet away. Barely breaking stride, and without a word, she stepped into his arms and placed her soft lips on his. She wasn't exactly sure what had gotten into her as she normally wouldn't have been so unabashed.

As the kiss broke, Ray smiled, flushed with surprise. "Well, hello to you, too." His index finger caressed one of her earrings. "Nice."

"Wore them just for you."

Ray pulled her in for another kiss then took her hand and led her into the store.

As the store's bell chimed when Reilly and Ray entered, the shoppe's clerk looked up from behind a large box of bowling shoes that sat on the checkout counter. With long scraggy hair, and a goatee, Doug – as his nametag identified him—looked like a cartoon in human form. *Vinnie must have the day off.*

"Who donates *bowling shoes*?" Doug asked them as they approached the checkout counter. "There isn't a bowling alley around here for a hundred miles."

Neither Reilly nor Ray could muster more than a shrug and a shake of the head in agreement with the man's confusion.

"They smell like feet, too," Doug continued, "and not in a good way." Again, the two had no response.

Reilly got the impression that Doug didn't have many people to talk to due to a lack of customers and probably spent much time having out-loud conversations with himself.

He picked up the box of clown-like shoes and dropped them onto the floor. After they landed with a crack and a cloud of dust, he adopted a more retail-like tone and said with a smile, "How may I help you today?"

"I'm looking for an outfit for my friend here." Reilly pointed at Ray who gave a small wave.

As Doug's thick prescription-assisted eyes focused on Ray, a spark of recognition was visible. "Hey! You're Ray Mitchell! You went to Carlin High, right? We went to school together!"

The blank, doll-like look in Ray's eyes betrayed his utter cluelessness. He had no idea who this guy was.

Doug did his best to refresh Ray's memory. "Dougie LaFontaine. I was the mascot for the volleyball team."

Reilly immediately tried to imagine what that mascot costume would have been. *A giant spongey piece of mistletoe with a face cut out of it?*

"I broke my coccyx during the half-time performance at the county semi-finals," Dougie continued.

Reilly could see that the vague memory of Dougie was coming back to Ray, but it was foggy, at best. Nevertheless, he managed a feeble, "Oh, yeah. *Dougie*. Of course. Great to see you."

There was an awkward beat of not-knowing-what-else-to-say smiling and nodding before Reilly jumped in with, "We're going to take a look around."

"Be my guest," Doug said, with a toothy smile.

Throughout the store's racks and racks of orphaned clothing, all impressively organized into sections—suits, jeans, dresses, blouses—there was a faint incense of moth-balls with an aftertaste of musty dust.

"So...where do we start?" Ray asked.

The way he dragged his feet spoke volumes. He wanted to get this over with as expeditiously as possible. "Well, we've got to find an outfit that matches your personality."

Ray gave her a sideways glance. "And what exactly is that?"

"Stylish but not too slick. And with a lot of character."

Ray nodded, satisfied with her description of him. "Sounds like me, all right."

"Why don't you park yourself by the changerooms, and I'll pull some options for you."

"You don't think I'm capable of making some selections for myself?"

Reilly could only answer with complete honesty. "Probably not but knock yourself out."

He replied with only a game-on grin.

Minutes later, she sat outside the ragged curtain change room, waiting for Ray to emerge in the first outfit she'd chosen. She had been impressed with all the various hidden gems she found throughout the store.

As Reilly sat patiently as Ray changed, she heard a familiar, honey-coated deep bass voice coming through the radio playing on the store's sound system. *Jingle Radio 191—dedicated to Christmas music 24/7. Yule love it.* It was Mr. Baritone himself.

As the overhead music played the next song, with the singer cooing, *Hurry down the chimney tonight...* Ray stepped out from behind the curtain in his first outfit.

It was a tweed suit, complete with elbow patches and a fedora. He looked like something out of a Sherlock Holmes novel. Reilly shook her head, nixing it right away. Next, he appeared wearing a baby blue tuxedo. He looked like a high school prom nightmare.

As she waited for option three, Doug pulled up a chair and sat beside her to take in the show. Ray's third outfit was a white dinner jacket with a black bow tie. He looked just like Bogart in *Casablanca.* It was a darn good look, but Reilly decided it was pushing the envelope a little.

Ray hardly even got past the curtain before his next outfit was shot down—a paisley candy cane suit. With simultaneous shakes of their heads, Reilly and Doug sent Ray changing again. As several more outfits were complete duds, Reilly was beginning to worry that they'd hit a wall.

Those concerns were completely blown away when Reilly laid eyes on Ray in his final outfit: a 60s-era, classic black suit, with a white shirt, matching pocket square, and a skinny tie. Reilly drew a sharp breath in, and a tingling sensation worked its way up her body. There was no better way to describe Ray than to say he was altogether dashing. He looked like JFK which was a very good thing. As he waited, Reilly slowly nodded her head. Their work here was done.

"You approve?"

The flushed expression on Reilly's face answered him. "I approve." She approached him and put her hands on his tie. "Except this knot should be a half-Windsor." Reilly was about to re-do the knot when Ray stopped her.

"I'm a grown man," he said with mock bravado, "I can tie my own tie." With that, he stepped back into the change room and closed the curtain with an abrupt, cocky swish.

A smile played on Reilly's lips as she waited for a moment. Then the curtain swished open again. "I lied," Ray admitted, "I have no idea how to tie a half-Windsor."

Reilly pushed Ray into the change room and stood close to him as she redid the tie. From this close, he looked even more scrumptiously dapper. It was remarkable what the right outfit on the right man could do.

"So... does this outfit match my personality?" he asked softly.

Reilly was so close to him she could feel his sweet, warm breath on her. "Perfectly." She tried to focus on tying the tie. "Simple, yet elegant."

Ray's chin quivered. "Simple?"

Reilly giggled, "Poor choice of words. How 'bout timeless?"

"Much better." Reilly couldn't hold herself back any longer and pulled him in for a much-needed kiss. Though it hadn't been long since their last kiss, it felt like forever. At that moment, the overly helpful Doug appeared with another tie option.

"I also found this burgundy tie, if you..." Realizing he'd interrupted the intimate moment, Doug blushed a bright Rudolph's nose red. "As you were." He then vanished. Reilly and Ray chuckled.

As they walked hand-in-hand out into the fluffy snowflake-filled Main Street, Ray carried his new suit on a hanger over his shoulder.

With the brisk, late-afternoon winter wind chilling their flushed faces, Ray slid his hand up the small of Reilly's back and up around her shoulder. With his steady, directional walking pace, Reilly realized he was leading her somewhere.

"Where to now?"

"I've got a surprise for you." He winked.

Chapter 16

The Old Sod was a beloved, ramshackle old Irish pub nestled in an alcove two streets off Mistletoe Lake's main drag.

As Ray led her toward the pub's front door, she could already hear that loud, buzzy din of the crowd inside.

He opened the red and brass-handled door for her, and her nose was instantly filled with the mild, not unpleasant redolence of beer, deep fried food, and close-quartered humans.

They made their way through the labyrinth of the crowd and found a small table for two in the back and took a seat. Catching a passing waitress with a tray of empties on her way back to the bar to fill up, Ray asked Reilly what she'd like to drink.

Figuring this wasn't exactly the kind of establishment where you might request to see the wine list, Reilly replied, "A beer of some kind."

Ray held up his pointer and middle fingers to the waitress and said, "Two pints, please."

The twentysomething girl nodded without breaking stride toward her destination.

"Busy," Reilly said loudly so Ray could hear her, despite only being a couple of feet away.

"Karaoke night."

On the small stage set up in the middle of the room, Topher stepped up and took the microphone. He was dressed for the occasion with slicked back hair, groomed sideburns, big Elvis shades, and two buttons undone on his collared shirt, showing off that thick gold chain. He was clearly the emcee for the evening.

"Welcome to Christmas karaoke night, folks!" Topher even sounded a little like Elvis as he waved his hand at the full band behind him. "Now, remember, this is what's called freestyle karaoke, meaning not only do you have to pick your song, but you also have to pick the *style* of music you want to sing. My go-to is always Elvis." He then couldn't resist adding, "Thank you, ladies and gentlemen. *Thankyouverymuch.*"

"As always, our house band *The Nobodies* will be here to back you up. Let's give them a round of applause."

There was a hearty hoot and holler from the crowd for the band, a ragtag collection of two women and two men who looked like the cottage-country, garage band version of *The Mamas and The Papas.*

Reilly mentally dug her heels in right there and then. There was *no way* she was going to get up on that stage.

"You like karaoke?" Ray asked her as the waitress placed two frothy, still settling pints of Guinness on their table.

"I like *listening* to karaoke." Reilly did her very best to be as clear as possible. "But I am *not* getting up on that stage," she added, even while knowing that such declarations were the kiss of death in situations like these—like a character in a war movie who makes the mistake of showing a picture of his sweetheart back home before getting killed in the very next scene.

Ray nodded in vigorous agreement, "I feel exactly the same way. We are *purely* audience members this evening."

Then came Topher's amplified voice from the stage. "Are my eyes deceiving me, or is that Ray Mitchell in the crowd?"

All eyes in the place turned toward their table. It was like being stared at by a herd of cattle. Ray raised his hand and gave a genteel wave.

A pitch of delight entered Topher's voice. "Well, ain't this quite the honor! We haven't seen you in here for ages."

Reilly hated where this exchange was going. Topher looked to the crowd, riling them up like any self-respecting karaoke emcee should. "Who wants to hear our very own Ray Mitchell kick off the evening with our first song?"

The crowd answered in the affirmative with a collective deafening roar. Ray good-naturedly raised his hands and shook his head declining the invitation, but this only caused the room to turn up their enthusiasm to eleven. They started pounding tables and chanting, "RAY! RAY! RAY! RAY!"

Reilly started looking for the nearest exits. Ray turned to her. "I don't think we're getting out of this." Her eyes rounded to saucers as she shook her head.

"No, no, no, no, no, no. *You're* not getting out of this. Nobody asked me to sing."

"You can't bail on me now." And without waiting for a response, he grabbed her hand and led her to the stage. The crowd went wild.

Ray took the mic from Topher and greeted the crowd. "Good evening." They answered with another collective cheer. Ray then motioned to Reilly. "I'm going to be doing a duet with Ms. Reilly Shore."

Everybody gave Reilly a very warm welcome while she stared at Ray like a buck in the middle of the freeway staring down an oncoming 18-wheeler.

Duet?

Ray gave her a wink. He seemed more comfortable with all this than he should have been. *Did he have this planned out all along?* Ray then turned to the band and said, "Let's do a heavy metal version of *Jingle Bells.*"

The stoic band nodded, and the lead guitarist began to play the opening of the song in loud metal power chords.

The rest of the band joined in, and Ray began to sing, "Jingle Bells, Jingle Bells, Jingle All the Waaaaaaaaay!" He then pulled Reilly in, and they shared the microphone for the next verse,

"Oh, what fun it is to ride in a one horse open sleeeeeeeigh!" At this, the crowd roared their approval. With the overwhelming endorsement, Reilly relaxed and gave in to the experience.

After finishing the song, they both bowed.

Topher took the mic back. "WOW! That was incredible. Who wants these two to do an encore?"

Everybody in the pub chanted, "ENCORE! ENCORE! ENCORE!" Ray and Reilly looked at each other and shrugged. *Why the heck not?*

Over the next thirty minutes, they commandeered *The Old Sod's* karaoke night to the delirious approval of everyone present. With each Christmas carol they sang, they went through the lexicon of different musical genres—a country and western version of *Silent Night,* an opera version of *We Wish You A Merry Christmas,* a reggae version of *Oh, Christmas Tree,* and a 70s disco version of *The Twelve Days of Christmas,* with Ray superbly hitting the *Bee Gees* falsetto notes.

By the time their set was done, they returned to their table to find it filled with drinks bought for them by their adoring fans. Being a rock star hadn't explicitly been on Reilly's bucket list, but, nonetheless, she could now cross it off.

Still floating from their performance, they picked up one of the many glasses in front of them and clinked. "I had no idea you could sing so well."

"Neither did I." She was pretty confident singing in the shower. But in front of an audience was a whole different story.

"This is the kind of thing that you don't often get in the city." Reilly looked around at the hometown gathering of people. "I love how real it all feels."

Ray nodded. Reilly could see a thought behind his eyes.

"What?"

"Nothing…it's just, you put such a high value on authenticity. Yet, your job…" He paused.

Despite his polite intention, the mention of the topic gave Reilly a queasy feeling. She knew what he was going to say next.

"Isn't home staging the *opposite* of authentic? You create the *illusion* of a home in a place where nobody actually lives, right?" By his gentle tone, Reilly got the sense that he wasn't intentionally being critical of her.

Reading her reaction, Ray backtracked. "I'm sorry. I didn't mean to be rude. I obviously don't know what I'm talking about."

"No, it's fine. In fact, you're absolutely right." She took another swill of her beer, surprised to see it almost half gone. "Home staging isn't where I started out. I got into interior design so I could create homes for people and give them an experience I never had in my own life. But when the trend of home staging took off, we saw the opportunity and went with it."

"If it's not making you happy, then why not go and do something that does?" Ray asked.

Again, it was an honest, innocent question, which made Reilly that much more uncomfortable. "I've thought about it, but my sister and I are a little bit in over our heads at the moment."

Their conversation was interrupted by Dougie from the thrift shop on stage where he was doing a horrendous rap version of *Deck The Halls*.

"I better go check in with Emma." Ray pulled out his phone and excused himself from the table with a gentle caress of Reilly's hand.

As Reilly sat alone, listening to the performance on stage, her regular life back home, seemed very far away at this moment. And she was content with that.

"Well, well, well, that was some performance you gave us." Edward, all smiles, approached her table. "You should be on *American Idol* with that voice." He wore an expensive suit that somehow still managed to be ill-fitting. Another example of him having the money to buy things but not the taste to pick them.

Her spirits deflated. Edward wasn't on the list of people she wanted to see tonight.

"I wouldn't go that far."

"May I?" Edward indicated Ray's vacant seat and sat before getting an answer. He put his elbows on the table and dragged his chair forward. "I've decided to buy the boat."

A sense of discomfort swept over Reilly. "Congratulations."

Edward then leaned in, pushing his head forward like a turtle. "I want you to redesign it for me."

The comment hit her like a lightning bolt.

"Redesign?" she stuttered.

"Yes. *Completely.*" True to form, Edward was incognizant of anything but his own excitement.

"Oh, I don't know, Edward. Boats aren't really my area of expertise."

"Nonsense! You're a miracle worker. From a resale point of view, I'll most likely get a better return on my investment if I completely renovate it first."

All the color melted out of Reilly's face as she tried to catch up. "You're gonna resell it?" She heard her voice creak.

"Don't get me wrong," Edward continued, like a barrel over a waterfall, "the boat is nice and everything. But it's too out of style."

Reilly considered the irony of Edward criticizing something for its lack of style.

"If I can completely gut it and modernize it, with your help, of course, I'll probably double my investment when I flip it."

Reilly was blindsided. "But Edward...I thought you wanted to buy the boat so your family could enjoy it?"

"I do! For this year. Once the holidays are over, I'm gonna sell it to the highest bidder. Let's meet tomorrow to discuss options." He stood. "That boat is going to be unrecognizable when we're finished with it!"

As Edward walked away, Reilly looked over to see Ray through the window outside talking animatedly on the phone. By his wide smile, he seemed to be getting some very good news.

"Hey—" Edward said, returning to the table, "Is it supposed to be bad luck to rename a boat?"

"Re-name?" Reilly asked, barely audible. She still hadn't wrapped her head around Edward's plans.

"Ah, it doesn't matter." Edward shrugged. "I'm not superstitious anyway." He took a few steps backward and gave her a double finger point. "Talk tomorrow. There's some other stuff brewing, and I want to bring you up to speed on everything." He then spun on his heels and disappeared into the crowd.

Chapter 17

Ray and Reilly walked back to the boat. A night-time plunge in temperature caused icicles to form like jagged teeth on the railing along the marina. Ray had his arm snugly around Reilly's shoulders. But she didn't feel the cold. Edward's decision had numbed her sensations, except for the dread in the pit of her stomach.

Ray, on the other hand, had a bounce to his step.

They walked up the gangplank of the boat and stood on the deck under the blue, wispy winter moonlight. *The Emma* was fully decked out in its Christmas Festival decorations and was looking utterly magnificent. The joyous surroundings made Reilly feel all the more ill with apprehension. She glanced over at the frigid lake water below, viscous with ice. She would have preferred to throw herself in there than face Ray with knowledge of Edward's intentions spinning around in her mind like a tornado.

Ray stepped close to her. "I had a really great time tonight."

"I did, too," Reilly said, her voice barely above a whisper. And she truly did. It was an exceedingly magical day and evening. All of it, except for one part, which managed to ruin the whole thing.

The chyron ticker tape ran through her mind, echoing Edward's words. And everywhere she looked around the boat, those headlines got louder and louder.

As Ray moved in to kiss her, Reilly hesitated. He pulled back.

"You okay?"

"Yeah, it's just…" Reilly trailed off. *Should I tell him?*

Ray mistook her shift in mood and began to back off. "I'm taking things too quickly, aren't I?"

"No…" Reilly managed.

"I'm sorry I don't mean to. It's just that…" Ray drew a breath in, "I really like you. Every time I'm around you I feel like some kind of awkward teenager." Then he smiled. "In a good way."

His openness broke Reilly's heart all the more. "I feel the same." Another cavernous moment passed.

A tug-of-war went on in Reilly's heart. *It's not right to keep this from him.*

Finally, she spit out, "Listen, Ray—"

At that exact moment, Ray said, "I wanted to tell you—"

They both stopped.

Ray's eyes crinkled. "Sorry. You go first."

"No, please. What were you going to say?"

"When I called Emma from the bar, she told me she was contacted by Grafton Arts Academy." He paused, but that open book face of his couldn't hide that the news was very good.

"And?"

"She got in."

Reilly's heart filled with joy, and she threw her arms around him. "Ray, that's fantastic news! You must be so proud!"

"I am. Emma did this all by herself." He was the shining personification of proud fatherhood. "I don't even want to think about how much it's going to cost. The sale of the boat *has* to go through now. Otherwise, I'll have to start selling my organs."

Like a solar eclipse, the shadow of doom instantly passed over Reilly. *The boat.*

Ray's gaze scanned around the vessel. "Maybe I can convince Edward to let us come visit every Christmas. That way the boat won't be completely lost to us."

Ray looked back to Reilly who nearly had an aneurysm trying not to betray the toil of emotions going on within her.

"What did you want to tell me?"

Reilly bit the inside of her cheek so hard she could taste blood. "Oh... It was nothing, really. It can wait," she lied.

Ray's eyes searched her face. "You sure?"

"Yeah," Reilly said quickly before adding, "congratulate Em for me. She truly deserves it."

Another thick moment passed before Ray smiled, squeezed her hand, and said goodnight. Reilly helplessly watched him walk down the gangplank and disappear along the dock.

Once she was alone, the solitude and silence hit her like a truck. Looking around the boat, taking in all the family history in it was utterly devastating. Was this her fault? Was it some curse that she'd brought with her, this shadow of transience that she'd grown up with all her life, that now she'd somehow inflicted on Ray and his family?

Though the idea was far-fetched, in Reilly's worried mind it checked out. After all, Edward had come here because of her. Reilly stared at the photo on the wall, into the hopeful eyes of young Ray who stared back at her. Her mind was transported back to that Christmas morning decades ago when she had found out that she was going to be losing the one true home she'd allowed into her heart. And now, it was happening again to someone she loved.

Reilly sat as a quiet sob began its slow crawl up from the bottom of her heavy heart. With salty, watery eyes she looked out at the tranquil lake which stared back at her, emotionless.

The gentle, metallic TINK of something falling grabbed her attention. Instinctively, Reilly reached up and discovered that one of her earrings was missing. She looked around at her feet, but it was nowhere to be seen.

Panicking, Reilly got down on her hands and knees to try to find it. She searched and searched, as another sob burst through to the surface. With her chest heaving and rivers of tears running down her face, she desperately tried to find the earring. She *needed* to find it. Though in the moment, she wasn't consciously aware of it, it was a need that transcended the actual object but what it symbolically represented.

After several frantic moments, she finally gave up and crumbled to the floor. The earring was gone, swallowed up in the crevices of the vessel.

Chapter 18

When Reilly groggily answered her phone the next morning to the Edward's bright-and-bushy-tailed voice—she had forgotten what a farmer-like morning person he was—she quickly shot down his suggestion of meeting at the B&B out of fear of running into Emmaline. Reilly needed to deal with this head-on, and the chance of seeing her would have the potential of exacerbating the situation. However, aside from holding a clandestine rendezvous in a vacant lot miles out of town, which Reilly considered, her only other suggestion was to meet at *The Old Sod,* which, admittedly, could look even more suspicious.

She hadn't slept much that previous night, and when her anxiety finally capitulated to her exhaustion near dawn after a knock-down, drag-out twelve-round bout, the klaxon of her cell phone woke her up. Reilly felt as though she had emerged from heavy anesthetics after an operation. It was a miracle that she had the wherewithal to change the suggested meeting locale.

Entering the pub ten minutes early with her Ray-Bans pulled down, Reilly saw Edward was already there.

He greeted her with a big smile as Reilly's gaze darted around the room to see if there was anyone in the place who might recognize her. Though she had reason to be nervous about a meeting like this being misconstrued by a nosey local, she was also aware that she was perhaps being overly paranoid.

After all, she hadn't done anything wrong, except perhaps for a little lie of omission. But the feeling reinforced for her how high the stakes had gotten and how deeply her feelings had grown for Ray. This felt like something very real, and the last thing she would forgive herself for was screwing it up.

Reilly had barely been in the seat for fifteen seconds before Edward pushed his iPad across the table to her. He'd taken the liberty of ordering her a cup of coffee as well. She tore open a packet of granulated brown sugar, dumped it into the cup, and took a gulp. On the iPad was a *Pinterest* page filled with gaudy images of boat re-decorating ideas.

As Edward yammered on, across the bar Reilly caught a glimpse of a familiar face passing through on his way out the door. It was Topher. *Great.*

Thankfully, he didn't look in her direction as he lumbered out the door into the chilly, overcast late morning. Reilly had slightly slid down in her chair in an ineffectual attempt at not being seen, but Edward hadn't noticed.

"Also, what do you think of renaming the boat to the *Louis*itania? Like the *Lusitania,* except *Louis.* Because that's my last name," he over-explained.

Reilly looked at him levelly for a beat. "I get it." She took another moment, to give him the opportunity to say that he was joking. He wasn't.

"You do know that the *Lusitania* was torpedoed," Reilly said, her composure paper-thin.

"Right. Buzzkill."

"You could go all out and call it *Titanic.*" Reilly struggled not to let her facetiousness sound too cutting. But, once again, the comment's intent went over his head.

"I thought of that. But you don't think it would be too, *Hey, look at me*?" The question was posed without a hint of irony.

Reilly put Edward's iPad, with its screen filled with tacky photos, down on the table. "Edward, I'm sorry, but I want no part of this. That boat is a significant part of a family's history. And I can't be involved in taking advantage of someone's difficult financial situation in order to simply turn a profit."

Edward looked at Reilly for a moment. He might have been surprised by her strong stance, but he wasn't outwardly offended. Instead, he considered her concerns in a business-like manner. "I respect your decision," he said at last.

Reilly hoped that the discussion would end there, but, knowing Edward, she figured that was an impossibility.

"However, I think you're only viewing this from one perspective. I'm not taking advantage of anyone. Quite the opposite, in fact. I'm *helping* this family by taking the burden of the boat off their hands." There was a smile in his voice. "Besides, he's selling the boat," he continued reasonably. "If I don't buy it, someone else will. What difference does it make?"

"It makes a difference to me. And for what it's worth, I hope you'll reconsider gutting and redesigning it. Not only does it have a history, but you'll be hard-pressed to do better than the craftsmanship that has gone into that boat."

On the way over, Reilly hadn't planned what she was going to say, but the words coming out of her mouth were as succinct as anything she could have possibly prepared. It was from the heart.

Edward nodded with a look of disappointment. "I admire your principles."

Again, Reilly wished it was over but knew it wasn't. A guy like Edward didn't achieve the success he had by lying down and conceding in a negotiation, which, in his mind, was obviously what this was. "But you might want to reconsider," he said, with the confidence of a card player holding a royal flush. "This kind of a deal could set you and your business up for life."

"With all due respect, Edward, redesigning one boat isn't going to set me up for life." She was about to politely excuse herself when Edward hit her with a mischievous smile.

"I'm not talking about the boat." He took a slower-than-necessary sip of his coffee. "You know the entire Mistletoe Lake harbor is for sale, right?" There was an opportunistic glint in his eye that unnerved her.

"Yes."

"Unfortunately, I don't have that kind of money," he said.

Reilly breathed an inward sigh of relief. *Thank God.*

"But…" he continued, "I've just had a conference call this morning with a group of investors who are interested in upgrading the entire harbor."

Reilly tensed up again.

"We can put a resort in, excavate the lake to allow for bigger boats, more waterfront restaurants, even a big box store."

All the blood drained from Reilly's face. This couldn't be happening. "Who would want that?"

"A big box store?" Edward lightheartedly shrugged, "People who liked big boxes, I guess." The guy loved his ill-timed jokes.

"Edward…" Reilly tried to adopt a cautioning tone, "if you do that, Mistletoe Lake won't even be cottage-country anymore."

Edward breathed out like he was extinguishing a candle. "Cottage country is passe. You know what people want? They want South Beach."

Reilly instantly felt like she was in one of those dreams where she was screaming but nobody could hear. "If they want South Beach…they should go to South Beach."

Edward adopted the intonation of a sage psychiatrist. "Reilly, just please rethink your decision."

He clearly didn't mean to sound condescending, though it was difficult not to take it that way.

"Redesigning *The Emma* is just the first step. You know I don't do anything halfway. This deal is going to be *huge*, and I want you to be part of it."

Then a grin curved at the corners of Edward's mouth. "I don't want you to miss the boat." Like a curtain being pulled open, his face broke into a big, toothy smile.

Reilly looked at him, despondent.

"Get it?" Edward chuckled. "*Boat.*"

She just stared.

Chapter 19

The streets of Mistletoe Lake were apocalyptically deserted. Reilly felt like an unfortunate character in a zombie movie who hadn't gotten the memo. Perhaps the soggy weather had kept everyone inside as they'd opted to stay under the covers and have breakfasts in bed in front of cozy fires. At a time like this, Reilly found it ironically fitting that she'd be out here, alone in the cold.

The highlight reel of her conversation with Edward thudded through her head, a clump of twisted, wet laundry clunking around in a hapless dryer.

Lost in the scoria of her own thoughts, Reilly stared down at the wet pavement underneath each one of her squishy footsteps as she walked. When the pale gray, cracked sidewalk turned to uneven cobble, she knew she had arrived on Main Street. Looking up, she saw the town Christmas tree, standing stoically, adorned in its decorations, looking regal despite the drizzly weather.

Just the two of them in the town square, Reilly approached the bench nearest the giant pine, wiped the seat with the sleeve of her coat, and sat. The tears on her cheeks were camouflaged by the intermixed droplets of snow. Their only difference in sensation was their opposing temperature.

She sat for a long quiet moment, listening to the infinite patter of flurries hitting the ground.

Then, her phone cut through the stillness, emitting the first few bars of a song that caused her breath to catch in her throat. The song was *She's Like The Wind* by Patrick Swayze. In her entire life, Reilly had only ever assigned specific ringtones to two people: her sister and her ex-boyfriend Greg. The reason for this choice was that Reilly and Greg had met at an 80s party-themed party thrown by a friend of theirs.

Since their breakup, Reilly had purged most of the reminders of their dissolved relationship from her life. However, she had forgotten to change the ringtone. It hadn't really mattered anyway, due to their mutual non-communication agreement. Until now.

Reilly pulled out the phone and stared at the phone. As Patrick Swayze sang, *She's like the wind, through my tree, h*er finger hesitated over the Accept button. *Why is he calling now? Is there something wrong?* Finally, she forced herself to answer.

"Greg?" Reilly's pulse quickened.

"Hiya, Rei." There was a lingering pause, as though in making the decision to call her, Greg had forgotten to figure out what he wanted to say beyond hello.

"It's good to hear your voice," Reilly said. It was, too. She'd always found it odd how two people could spend years together inhabiting each other's lives, privy to all the intimate minutia of their day-to-day existence, and then, overnight, vanish from each other.

"I know we weren't talking and stuff, but I just wanted to call to make sure you were doing okay."

Reilly couldn't hear any sadness or longing in his voice. Instead of the lost little boy who wept the very last time they spoke, he now sounded as though he was on more emotionally solid ground. It warmed her heart. She didn't ask, nor did he mention it, but she could sense that his heartbreak had healed and that he'd moved on.

"Yeah, I'm doing okay," Reilly replied.

"That makes me happy." She heard the warmth in his tone. "I'm doing okay, too."

Reilly took this as Greg's way of saying he had made his peace with the dissolution of their love, too.

"I also wanted to say, Merry Christmas. I know it is your very favorite time of year." Greg's voice lifted.

"Merry Christmas to you, too."

The two said their goodbyes and then, just like that, he was gone. Once again alone, with only the Mistletoe Lake town Christmas Tree as her witness, Reilly said under her breath, into the ether, "Have a good life, Greg Darlington." And her heart was filled with bittersweet happiness.

Reilly was soaking by the time she'd gotten back to *The Emma*. As she stepped up onto the deck of the boat, she was surprised to see Ray climbing up from the engine room down below. She'd phoned him several times on the way over, only to be met with the stonewall of his voicemail after zero rings.

Ray had been trying to fix the motor again, as evidenced by his greasy hands which he wiped with a rag. "Sorry I let myself in, but you weren't here, and I needed to have another look at the engine."

Reilly pushed her wet hair back from her face. "Don't be silly. You can come aboard anytime you like. It's your boat."

"Not for long," he replied. Ray seemed off. Strange. He wasn't holding eye contact with Reilly.

"You okay?" The darkness of his mood made her uneasy.

"I've just spent the morning shopping online for alternators." He still avoided eye contact. "Even the used ones are expensive. That, on top of the bills and the upkeep of the boat, it's just too much."

"It's a good thing you have a buyer then."

He finally looked her dead in the eye. "Good for you, too."

Completely surprised by the blunt comment, Reilly's gaze searched his face.

"How is our friend Edward, anyway? I heard you had lunch with him today."

Reilly was totally caught off-guard.

"It's a small town," Ray said, anticipating her question, with a cold edge in his voice. "There's no such thing as a secret."

Topher, the town gossip.

"I didn't meet with Edward in secret," Reilly managed, taken aback.

"Well then, what were you talking about?" Reilly hesitated, about to answer, but he just kept barreling through, "After I left last night, I did a little research on our friend Edward Louis. Big real estate guy. Likes to gut houses and flip them." His intonation was curt, placing extra emphasis on those consonants. "That's the kind of work you did with him, isn't it?"

Reilly stared at him levelly. "Yes."

A pregnant beat that loomed with unpleasantness slid by like a slug. "He doesn't want to buy this boat for his family, does he?" Ray's lip curled with disappointment.

"No."

Ray couldn't hide the deep hurt in his eyes. "Did you know about his plans to redesign the boat?"

"I only found out last night. I wanted to tell you; I swear. You seemed so stressed about finances."

Ray tossed the greasy rag on a table. "Is he giving you a good commission at least?"

Reilly took a step closer to him. "Ray, I'm not working with him."

He sucked his lips against his teeth. "That's a little hard to believe. I mean, you've worked together in the past. Now you just *happen* to be in the same small town at Christmas? And, come to think of it, the very first day I met you was the first day I met him, wasn't it?"

"It's not how it looks," Reilly could only offer.

"Weren't you the one who inspired him to come to Mistletoe Lake? That's what he said, right?"

"I agree that it all seems very suspicious. But you've got to believe me."

"How can I? How can I trust that you're not just like all the other seasonals?" Hurt laced his voice.

Now Reilly pushed her way into his personal space, not allowing his eyes to divert from hers. "I wouldn't do that to you. I had lunch with Edward today to tell him that I wasn't interested in helping him change this boat. For what it's worth, I did my best to convince him not to change one thing. I know that I've only been on this boat for a few days, but the truth is…is that I've fallen in love with it."

Like a runaway train, the next words came out of her mouth without her really realizing, "And I've fallen in love with you, too, if you must know."

Reilly stood there, surprised at her own admission and vulnerable at the utter truth of it. Hearing her words, Ray instantly softened.

"I'm sorry," he said, "I shouldn't have accused you. You've done nothing but go out of your way to help every day." He moved closer to her. "It's been really stressful lately. But it's not your fault." He closed his eyes for a brief second. "Can you forgive me?"

Reilly slid her hands around his waist. "Of course." Ray sunk into her. "There's something else you need to know…" She took a heavy breath.

Before Reilly could continue, they heard a voice calling from the dock. A voice Reilly knew all too well.

"Hey, sis!"

As Tara galloped her way up the gangplank, overdressed in stylish city attire which especially stood out in the midst of lake country, she extended her hand to Ray.

"Hi. I'm Reilly's sister Tara." Reilly remained speechless as she stared at Tara who took an appraising look around the boat. "Oh, yeah. Once we give this thing a complete overhaul, the resale value is going to skyrocket." Reilly stood statue-still, wordlessly watching this catastrophe unfold in front of her.

"How was your lunch with Edward?" Tara asked Reilly, "It's so exciting, isn't it?"

"Tara—" Reilly tried to interrupt her sister, but that was near impossible in times like this.

"This harbor is going to look so different." Tara whistled as she looked out at the Mistletoe Lake pier. "Edward says he's already got a lot of the money lined up."

Ray looked as though he'd been hit by a taser. "What?"

"The guy who's buying your boat is also putting together a group of investors to revamp the entire Mistletoe Lake harbor." Tara declared obliviously. "Isn't that cool?"

Ray turned to Reilly; his gaze filled with shattering disappointment. And she knew then there was absolutely nothing she could say.

Chapter 20

Reilly and Tara walked back quickly along the creaky, frozen pier. Reilly carried her hastily packed suitcases in her cold, white-knuckled hands. The moment Ray had turned on his heel and left the boat was when she knew she had to go. Inside, she was a mess of topsy-turvy emotions.

"What was that all about?" Tara asked, with aloof curiosity.

"It's a family boat." Reilly could barely keep a lid on her charged emotions. "He's having a tough time with the idea of selling it."

"Well, if he doesn't want to sell it, why is he selling it?"

Plumes of Reilly's warm breath intermixed with the frigid air. "Because. It's complicated, Tara. Sometimes life is complicated. That boat is their home. This town is their *home*."

As with any other time that she saw her sister on the brink of freaking out, Tara remained calm and non-reactionary. "Why are you so upset? And why are you mad *at me*?"

Reilly stopped walking. "What are you doing here, Tara? I thought you were supposed to arrive tomorrow."

"I managed to get an earlier flight and I wanted to surprise you."

"Oh, please. You came here because you saw a business opportunity."

Tara wasn't rattled by the accusation. "Yes." There was no apology in her voice. "A huge business opportunity *for us.*" Tara emphasized the last part. "This is going to put us in the black for good."

Reilly didn't have the energy to argue with her. It was a deeply-rooted sister dynamic. "Where are you staying?" she asked instead, exasperated.

"The Sunset Inn. It's actually quite nice," The motel where they'd originally made their reservations. "I had them put a room aside for you, too, just in case."

Though the inn had been sold out when Reilly had asked, she didn't question how Tara had managed to get them rooms. Her sister had always had an uncanny skill of getting things that weren't available to regular people—tickets to concerts, VIP admission to nightclubs, dishes that weren't on the menu. That was just one of the things that made her a good businesswoman.

"What's going on with you? Does this have anything to do with that Ray guy? He's pretty cute."

Reilly sucked in a deep gasp of air, and the cold burned her lungs. "Look, I just need time to process everything. Go back to the motel. I'll meet you there later."

"Okay." Tara studied her for a moment. "You're *sure* you're okay?"

Reilly gave the question genuine consideration. "No." She handed her suitcase to Tara and walked away along the dock.

Numb with confusion and devastation, Reilly wandered down Main Street like she was in a waking, disjointed dream. She stopped outside the general store. It had seemed both lifetimes and blinkingly brief moments ago she'd first set eyes on the quaint store. She walked up to the display window where the idyllic model of the Christmas Harbor Festival was on display. Reilly stared at it longingly. If only the real-life version could be as uncomplicated.

Then she saw a face appear to her in the window from inside the store. It was Emma. Tears streaked her face.

Reilly entered the store and threw her arms around the little girl. "Are you okay?" Emma struggled to speak through her choking sobs.

"My dad got in touch with Edward this morning and told him he wants to sell the boat, as is." The girl took a breath, trying to get all the words out. "Edward agreed but asked if we could pull out of the competition so he could enter himself. My dad says he's got no choice."

A black canyon opened in Reilly's stomach, and the shattered pieces of her heart crumbled into it. "*What?*" This was even worse than she could have imagined. What had Edward been thinking?

"I know this is my fault because I got into the school." Emma's grief poured out in waves.

Reilly took Emma by the shoulders and looked deeply into her watery eyes. "This is *not* your fault, at all. Your dad is so proud of you. He'd do anything for you."

Emma nodded but remained quiet.

"And hey!" Reilly continued, desperate to find one bright spot in this obsidian gloom that had descended. "You got into Grafton Arts Academy! That's an incredible accomplishment! You deserve it. You're so talented."

"Thank you." Emma tried but failed to wipe her tears.

A sob rose in Reilly's throat, too. "I'm sorry for all the trouble I've caused you and your dad."

"You didn't cause us any trouble." Emma took her hand. Now, it was her turn to console Reilly. "You've already made it an unforgettable Christmas."

The two tearfully hugged for a long moment, as though they were trying to give each other the strength to let go of the connection that had so naturally and easily grown between them. Reilly had truly felt accepted into this family. And now she was faced with saying goodbye and being released back into the murky world. Her heart hadn't hurt like this in a long time.

"Merry Christmas, Em."

"Merry Christmas."

With a leaden heart, Reilly turned to walk out of the store. As she got to the door, Emma called to her, "Wait."

With an ember of hope in her heart, Reilly turned. Emma grabbed something from behind the store's counter and approached. It was a large shipping box. She handed it to her. "This arrived for you this morning."

Reilly took the box into her hands and looked at it. The thought of whatever was inside caused another wave of sadness to wash over her.

"Promise me that we'll keep in touch and stay friends?" Emma was always very mature for her age, but in this moment, she looked every bit the little girl that she was.

"Always."

Chapter 21

The Sunset Inn was a lonely building that sat on the edge of the freeway five miles outside of town. It wasn't as bad as the first impression Reilly had gotten when she'd passed the place at fifty-five miles per hour. The room was clean with running water and heat. As she wasn't in any position to be choosy, the motel would do just fine.

She needed a scalding-hot shower to melt away the chill in her bones. No matter how much the drizzly showerhead rained down steamy water on top of her, it couldn't wash away the despair inside her.

She pulled back the heavy, blackout curtains and looked out at the blanket of stars over Mistletoe Lake in the distance.

From her perspective, the lake's harbor looked like it was the size of a toy. It could have been the diorama that Reilly had helped Emma install in the display window of the general store.

Another flood of sadness rose in her as she thought about how that harbor would change once Edward's investors had gotten their hands on it. How it would lose its charm and become something trampled by the millions of footprints of humanity. Reilly had only set eyes on this hamlet a week ago, yet it had webbed its way into her heart. She felt protective of it.

And then, the slow orbit of a realization dawned on her. Under her breath, she said, "Deanewood."

The next morning, the freeway that crisscrossed in front of the motel was as busy as an abandoned bowling alley. Not even one car had left its tire tracks in the fallen snow. Reilly stood outside room six in the frigid morning sunlight and knocked with cold knuckles on the door. It took several attempts, each one louder than the previous, before Tara stomped across the floor and answered—first clanging the door's locked latch before opening it wide and staring, nonplussed at her older sister.

Her hair was a squirrel's nest of bed-headedness.

"Are you waking me up because it's Christmas Eve? If so, you might have just texted. As you may recall, I'm not a morning person."

"I've made a decision, and I need to talk to you about it because it affects both of us." The words spewed out of Reilly's mouth like a stampede of spooked horses

Tara stifled a yawn. "You're getting bangs."

"I'm quitting the home staging business," Reilly blurted.

"What?" The question had vaporized any lingering, cobwebby sleepiness. "Have you slept yet?"

"From now on, I'm going to focus on helping people create *homes*," Reilly continued, eager to share her revelation, but also a little apprehensive at how Tara would take it. "That was always my dream. It's why I got into this business in the first place."

Tara studied Reilly for several seconds. "Wait… Is this about Ray?"

Reilly didn't reply, but she didn't need to.

"You're in love with him, aren't you?" Again, the look on Reilly's face was the only answer Tara needed. "Oh my gosh. I'm so sorry. Here I was only thinking about business."

"It's not your fault. It's mine." Reilly quietly absolved her. "I haven't been honest with myself lately about what I want out of life. That ends right now."

Tara smiled and hugged her.

"Are you okay with this?"

"Of course," Tara assured her, "I just want my sister to be happy."

"But what about the company? And Edward's big business deal? Don't we need to get in on something like that?"

Tara shrugged, "Yes. But we'll figure something else out. We always do," she said with that innate businesslike assuredness. "As long as you never lose your passion, we'll always be fine."

In that moment, Reilly felt more love for her sister than she could ever remember having before.

"After all," Tara continued, "you're the creative engine behind the company. I'm just the numbers person."

"I love you."

"Ditto," Tara replied, before turning on her heel and traipsing back to bed.

Chapter 22

The taxi driver hadn't even come to a full stop before Reilly jumped into the car.

"I don't mind," he'd said when Reilly had remarked how thankful she was that he'd agreed to come all the way out to The Sunset Inn on the edge of town on Christmas Eve, no less. "I don't have any family anymore since my wife, Estelle, died two years back. Driving a cab gets me out of the house and gives me a chance to chit-chat with nice folks such as yourself," the man said, his milky blue eyes glancing at her in the rearview. "Cuts the loneliness. Especially at the holidays."

Reilly had noticed that he had a Tupperware container of macaroni and a neatly folded newspaper on the passenger seat beside him. She pictured him, alone in his house preparing his lunch to bring with him on his shift, and it broke her heart a little bit.

"You here for the Christmas Harbor Festival?" he asked.

Without the energy or time to go into the intricate details, she simply replied, "I sure am."

"You're in for a real treat. It's a truly spectacular sight. The kinda thing that gives me hope at this time of year."

As the cab made its way through the deserted town street, the driver said that this year's festival was going to be extra special. "There's a boat in our harbor; it's called *The Emma*. It belongs to Desmond Mitchell's boy. It was one of the very first boats ever to grace our little marina."

Reilly's heart quickened as he recounted the story to her that she knew all too well. "*The Emma* hasn't been part of the festival for as far back as I can remember. But this year Ray is gonna enter it. Lord knows what changed his mind, but it's caused a bit of excitement for all us locals. We're all pulling for him."

Reilly suddenly noticed that the driver hadn't turned on the taximeter. When she questioned it, he kindly waved his hand. "No charge today. Merry Christmas."

Sprinting along the dock, Reilly saw Ray standing on the deck of *The Emma*. As their eyes met, she said breathlessly, "Can we talk?" Without waiting for a response, she ran up the gangplank onto the deck of the boat.

"This boat is Deanewood, the house that I loved when I was growing up. The one that I lost," she exclaimed.

Ray's face was a mask of unreadable impassiveness, but Reilly didn't let that deter her. She leaned into the propulsion of her enthusiasm. "But at least I have the memory of that Christmas there. *The Emma* is the same kind of place for you. Home. And I can't just stand by and let you lose it without having a proper last Christmas here."

Without saying a word, Ray allowed a look of regret to pass through his eyes, before glancing past Reilly over her shoulder. Following his gaze, Reilly turned to see...they were not alone.

Edward was there. Emma and Emmaline were, as well, wearing dour expressions on their faces. On the table in front of Edward was a thick, typed document with several neon yellow *sign here* arrow stickers poking out of it.

All eyes were on Reilly. She hesitated, not expecting to have an audience for what she wanted to say to Ray. But she soldiered on, turning back to Ray.

"I know you feel as though I've betrayed you. You don't have to forgive me if you don't want to." Reilly locked in on his eyes, unrattled that he was still giving her nothing. "But can I ask you one thing?" She pleaded. "Please don't withdraw the boat from the Harbor Festival. For your family."

"Reilly…" Ray said, hanging his head, "as far as the boat is concerned, you'll have to ask Edward. He's the rightful owner now. That boat is sold."

Shocked, Reilly spun back and took another look at the papers on the table. Sure enough, next to each of those arrow stickers were Ray's signatures. The high hopes that Reilly had entered with immediately plummeted.

Numb, she turned and looked at Ray who still couldn't meet her gaze. "But…what about you wanting the boat to be preserved?"

Ray slowly shook his head, "I can't rightfully tell Edward what to do with the boat. He can scuttle it and let it sink to the bottom of the lake if he likes."

Edward did his best to diffuse the rising tension with a joke. "Sink it like the *Lusitania*? I guarantee you that I'm not going to do that." The bad joke bombed. Everyone just stared at him

"Besides, what difference does it make?" Ray continued with a funereal tone. "From the sound of it, this whole town will be unrecognizable soon anyway."

Reilly could see the defeat in Ray. She looked to Emma who screamed for help with her eyes. All the beautiful Christmas decorations on the boat now seemed so tragic. A cruel joke.

Then, seized with a last-ditch idea, Reilly turned to Edward. "Edward, as the new, rightful owner, would you be willing to let me fulfill my promise to Emma and her family to have one last Christmas on the boat? You can take possession at exactly one minute past midnight after the party."

With everyone staring at him expectantly, Edward shifted uncomfortably. "Well…I really wanted to enter into the festival myself this year." Reilly stayed silent, holding firm. It was a negotiating tactic she'd picked up from him. "But…" Edward continued "I suppose I can't refuse you after all you've done for me in the past."

"Thank you."

"I have another request," Emma said, stepping forward. She now had the floor. "I only want the boat to be part of the festival, if you'll agree to take part, too," she said to her dad. There was a tremble of emotion in her voice. "I love this boat," Emma continued, fighting back tears. "But the reason I do is that it means I get to spend time with you and Nana. The Harbor Festival doesn't mean anything to me unless you're there. Promise you'll come?"

Ray's eyes were glassy. His mouth sagged, as though he were repressing a sob. "I promise."

Chapter 23

Christmas Eve gracefully descended on Mistletoe Lake. With dueling supernovas of excitement and dread roiling in her stomach, Reilly clicked along the pier in her Christmas red, strappy Jimmy Choo heels, last year's Christmas present from her sister. Tara bought them for Reilly knowing that her overly pragmatic older sister would never splurge on something so extravagant for herself.

In Reilly's hands was the large box that Emma had handed to her at the General Store. She'd spent a large portion of her afternoon gift-wrapping it. Though she was a Christmas aficionado, she was surprisingly untalented at wrapping gifts. This gift, however, she needed to get right. After several botched attempts and near nosebleed-worthy rounds of concentration, Reilly was okay with the result which looked surprisingly professional.

With every step Reilly took along the creaky wooden dock, the sound of the party on the deck of *The Emma* got louder. From her perspective, the boat looked utterly dazzling. As she arrived at the gangplank leading up to the deck, she saw all the guests in evening attire mingling about. She stood there for a moment, admiring all the work the three of them had put into decorating *The Emma*. It was breathtakingly gorgeous. Though her heart was a leaden anchor, at least for tonight, to have the boat shine in all its glory, it would all be worth it.

Well, maybe.

Reilly took a big, nervous breath and made her way up onto the deck. As she moved through the crowd, she saw several familiar faces—locals whom she'd encountered over the last week, even just via a friendly passing wave—as well as many faces she didn't recognize at all. *They must be the seasonals.* She wondered which category she fell into now. Perhaps neither, instead precariously standing with a foot in both worlds.

As she arrived at the tree sitting centerstage on the deck, the very same one she and Emma had worked so diligently decorating, Reilly placed the gift underneath, amongst the handful of others. She straightened the bow on the box and made sure the card was visible. On the envelope in her neatest penmanship, she'd written simply, *"For Ray."*

"Enjoying the party?" Reilly heard, and she turned to see Edward standing in front of her. He was wearing yet another over-priced, under-stylish suit. *No surprise.*

"I've only just arrived," Reilly said, finding it difficult to be completely polite.

"Well, it's wonderful." Edward beamed. "Just wonderful. Made more so by the way you have decorated the boat."

"Thank you." There was an undertone of awkwardness in her voice.

Edward took a step nearer to her. Reilly prepared herself for another armada of arguments about how she should reconsider working with him to redesign the boat.

"I must say, I feel a little awkward about yesterday," he said, instead, surprising her. "The last thing I would want to come across as is the bad guy."

Edward looked sincerely troubled. It wasn't as though he was some cutthroat, unfeeling person. But he was a successful businessman. Concerns about personal likeability were not usually a prominent characteristic of the successful and wealthy.

"I don't think anyone feels that way, Edward." It wasn't *entirely* true, but more than a half-truth. *Three quarters?*

"I certainly hope not. It's nothing personal, after all. Just business."

Reilly never understood why that was such a ubiquitous allegory that people clung to. In her experience, the two were almost always interconnected, like conjoined twins.

"I just love the feeling I get when I'm here. In this town. It just feels so…" He trailed off as if searching for the right word.

"Authentic?"

"Yes! That's exactly it."

Chapter 24

Alone again, Reilly scanned the deck. On the opposite end, near the boat's stern, she saw Ray sitting with Emmaline and Emma. Ray was dressed impeccably in his new vintage suit. Emmaline looked quite elegant wearing a long black velvet dress with matching hat and gloves. Emma wore an adorable, red and white dress. With the colorful Christmas lights all around, the three were the picture of style and grace.

They sat silently watching their guests merrily wassailing in intersecting currents around the deck of the boat. Reilly took a nervous breath in and approached them.

Without noticing her, Emma turned to Emmaline. "I feel like Grandpa is here with us right now. Don't you, Nana?" Emmaline's eyes welled with emotion as she looked up at the framed photo of Ray and Desmond taken decades before, hanging on the wall. From such a different time. A different *lifetime,* almost. "I do." From the short distance between them, Reilly could see the look of nostalgia on the older woman's face.

Reilly felt awkward approaching, eavesdropping on this family moment, but to turn and slink away would be even odder. So, she just stood there, hoping she'd remain hidden in plain sight amongst the other party guests moving around her.

"I'm so sorry about all of this. I guess I was so preoccupied with doing the right thing for my family, that I lost sight of what was really important. And, in spite of it all, I *still* lost the boat," Ray said to his mother and daughter.

Both Emmaline and Emma put their arms around him. "You didn't lose the boat," Emmaline said. "None of this is your fault. And the most important thing—more than anything else in this world—is that we three are together." She took one of each of their hands in hers. "That's what your father would have wanted more than anything."

She looked out over the boat's deck to the Mistletoe pier, spanning across the lakeshore. "And, as for this old town, maybe a facelift is exactly what it needs. I could say the same for myself." She looked at Emma, who smiled in spite of her melancholy.

"What do I always say?" Emmaline asked.

With a voice trembling with emotion, Emma replied, "You can't blame the world for changing."

"With all the beauty there is in the world, some of it is the kind that made you sad. However, that didn't make it less beautiful."

The three sat for another lingering moment, contemplating the unknowable future. Then, Emma looked up and saw Reilly standing there like a statue. The little girl smiled and nudged her dad.

"Dad? I think there's someone here to see you."

Ray's gaze followed Emma's where he saw Reilly. She was bathed in the warm, glowing light of the Christmas tree.

With wisdom born of age, Emmaline held out her hand to Emma. "Shall we go mingle?"

"You bet." The two left Reilly and Ray alone.

In the middle of all the revelers on the boat, Reilly and Ray stood and looked at each other as though they were the only two people there.

"Hi," Reilly said, unable to think of something more interesting to say.

"Hi." They stood for another moment, neither moving.

"The boat looks gorgeous," he added. "You do, too."

"You're looking very handsome yourself." Reilly felt a little like a little kid trying unsuccessfully to sound like an adult.

"I have a good stylist." They shared a small smile.

"I'm sorry for the things I said. I shouldn't have overheated the way I did."

Once again, his heart opened like a book to her. "It's okay. You've been going through a lot."

He shook his head. "Still. It's no excuse. Without you, we wouldn't have had such a beautiful last Christmas here. My father would have been very proud."

Reilly wanted to fold herself into him. But the energy had shifted so quickly over the last eighteen hours, that she didn't know where she stood in his heart.

They heard the click of heels across the varnished wood floor coming toward them. Reilly turned to see Tara approaching.

"Hey, Sis." She smiled.

Reilly turned to Ray. "You remember my sister, Tara."

"How could I forget?"

"I apologize if I seemed insensitive the other day," Tara continued to Ray with sincerity. "I hope you know that I'm not the kind of person who would get in the way of my sister and the guy she's in love with."

Though her sister had a chronic tendency of disappearing deep into the People's Republic of Tara where she couldn't see past the end of her own nose, Reilly also knew that she only wanted the best for her. And she also knew that Tara loved to stir the pot by dropping Love-word bombs and putting Reilly on the spot.

After an awkward, lingering beat, Tara smiled. "Well, I guess I'll go get myself a drink. Maybe track down Edward."

She didn't need to track down Edward. She'd instantly found him and had been clocking him throughout their conversation.

Alone again, Reilly and Ray locked eyes.

"In love with, huh?" He was trying to sound cool, with his crooked smile, like a male lead in a romantic movie, but Reilly heard the honesty of the question bleeding through in his voice.

"I'm afraid so," Reilly confirmed from her heart.

Ray's crooked smile evened out fully. "Well, then, I guess we're in the same boat."

Reilly shook her head and chuckled. "Dad joke." They kissed, and it felt even better than the very first time. Reilly then intertwined her fingers around the palm of his hand. "I got something for you."

Reilly led him, weaving through the crowd, to the Christmas Tree. Up close, the plethora of decorations on it was intense. She and Emma may have gone a little overboard on it. If Cleopatra were a Christmas Tree, this would be it.

Reilly picked up Ray's gift and handed it to him. As the party had just entered its full swing stage, it probably wasn't the right time to be handing out gifts, but she couldn't wait. She'd always been like that. That's why she always did her gift shopping on Christmas Eve.

Ray took the large box into his hands and tore through the perfect wrapping job she had spent so much of her day trying to get right.

When Ray saw what was underneath—a box containing a gleaming piece of machinery—he sucked in a sharp breath. Reilly grinned. This was exactly the kind of feeling she loved to see people experience. It was the same when she brought clients into their re-decorated homes for the first time.

"A new alternator," he said in awe.

"As I recall you needed one." And it had been quite a rigamarole getting it delivered on time.

"Thank you."

Reilly could see the swirl of thoughts and emotions within him, all overlapping.

"I ordered it before the boat was sold," she said quickly.

"It's a beautiful gift," he said.

There was a small stage set up at the bow of the boat's deck. Topher, in an authentic Aloha from Hawaii white bell-bottomed suit, stood on stage at the microphone.

"Alright, ladies and gentlemen. Let's kick this party up a notch or two. Who's ready for some Christmas karaoke?" Topher bellowed over the microphone. The crowd cheered.

The band began to play a bluesy rendition of *Have Yourself a Merry Little Christmas* as Topher sang in an Elvis twang.

Ray raised an eyebrow, but before he could even open his mouth, Reilly quashed any idea he might have. "I'm not singing tonight, Ray. If that's what you're about to ask. You already tricked me into that once."

He laughed. "Okay, fine. I promise." He took her hand. "Would you like to dance instead?"

Now, it was Reilly's turn to sound like the *female* lead in a romantic movie. "Thought you'd never ask."

He guided her out to the middle of the dance floor. Putting his hand on the small of her back, he pulled her close and gently rested his cheek against hers. Their bodies began to move in unison to the music. As other couples moved to join them, Reilly closed her eyes. Ray's slow, steady pulse kept time with the music, his breath caressing the back of her neck.

Beyond the bubble of *The Emma*, the night had won its battle against the last vestiges of the daylight, bringing with it a deep, December chill. But, blanketed in this moment, Reilly felt the warmth of home. As she opened eyes, she saw her sister and Edward embraced in a slow dance as well. Reilly smiled. All that bluster from Tara about not having a crush on Edward paled in comparison to the giddiness she saw in her sister's eyes as the two moved to the music in a close embrace.

Later, she and Ray found a private spot on the starboard side of the boat. He kept his arm around her waist as they sipped from glasses of rose prosecco.

Ray looked out at the tired pier of Mistletoe Lake, which stood like an old man who was now but a shadow of the virility of his youth. "I lied," Ray whispered.

The lights on the boat's deck reflected in his dark eyes, but his face remained expressionless. Before Reilly could ask him to elaborate, Ray reached into his jacket and took out a Christmas gift that looked like it had been wrapped by a three-year-old. Just further confirmation for Reilly that Ray was a fellow after her own heart.

"I couldn't let Christmas go by without getting you something," Ray said, with a slight childlike bashfulness. "It's nothing super special so don't get your hopes up."

Reilly tore open the haphazardly wrapped paper.

"*Mistletoes! Exactly* what I wanted!" She held the pair of cozy footy socks from the novelty section of the General Store in her hand. It was a perfect gift.

"Thank you."

Ray's eyes crinkled. "I got you something else, too. Well, I didn't *get* it for you so much as found it." Ray pulled out Reilly's missing Christmas heart earring from his pocket.

Seeing it, she gasped. "Where did you find it?"

"Somewhere in the nooks of the boat as I was cleaning it out. Figured you'd want it back." He held the single earring up to her ear and smiled.

Reilly opened her clutch and took out its matching counterpart. "I brought it just in case." She put both earrings on. If nothing else, they matched her outfit.

"What do you think?"

"I think you're perfect."

Reilly moved in close and gave him a soft kiss on the lips.

"Are you going to be okay?" she asked gently. She didn't need to be told that his soul was still heavy.

"I think so." Ray blinked stoically as he glanced back out at the harbor. "I just can't believe that all of this is going to be gone soon."

"You don't know that for sure." Reilly tried to inject a little hope into his mood.

"Yes, I do. It's been slowly slipping away for years. This is just the final straw."

He was probably right. There wasn't much else Reilly could say. She put her head on his shoulder, and they stood quietly for several moments as the party hummed behind them.

"Such a wonderful evening." The two turned around as Edward approached, handing them each a fresh flute of prosecco. "I'm so happy to have the opportunity to celebrate with you." His cheeks were flushed from drinks and dancing. "And I must say *The Emma* is the perfect venue."

Reilly hadn't thought about the time until that moment. She'd forgotten the hasty deal she'd made with Edward about him taking possession of the boat at one minute past midnight. They must have been within two hours of that now when the boat would turn into a pumpkin. A pumpkin Ray no longer officially owned.

"Well, the boat is almost yours. Then you can throw as many parties on it as you like," Ray said, not in a best-man-has-won concession.

Edward nodded, not giving anything away. "That would be nice." He then smiled with excitement. "But *I* won't be the one hosting them."

Reilly didn't know where Edward was going with this. Was it possible he'd already found another buyer for the boat—someone to buy it *after* he bought it and fixed it up? Even though she and Edward had had a heart-to-heart earlier when she'd first arrived at the party, with a wheeler-dealer like he was, she wouldn't put it past him. He was also capable of gleefully making this announcement while being completely oblivious to the sensitivity of the situation. She braced herself for the worst.

As Ray looked at Edward for clarification, Edward pulled out the boat's sale contract from the inside pocket of his jacket. With a grin that practically stretched around to the back of his head, he tore up the documents—first in half, then in quarters, then in eights—until it was nothing more than a ragged paper-doll collection covered in legal jargon.

Ray and Reilly's puzzlement graduated to sheer shock. Nearby, Reilly caught sight of Emma who had been eavesdropping on this conversation—and perhaps on Reilly and her dad all evening. The awe of Edward's surprise was etched on her face, too.

"After the wonderful time I've had here tonight, I simply couldn't live with myself knowing I was responsible for taking this boat away from you and your family." Edward let the torn pieces of the contract fall to the floor like confetti. "Besides the boat is your home. It should stay that way." He then winked at Reilly. "You can't put a price on authenticity."

Still commanding the moment, Edward gestured out to the Mistletoe Lake harbor. He wasn't finished bestowing his Christmas cheer on them. "That goes for this entire place. I'm pulling the plug on the whole business proposal to purchase the Mistletoe Lake Harbor." He gave Ray a goofy grin. "Instead, I'm gonna donate the money I was going to use to buy your boat to the town municipality, so they don't have to sell, either."

Ray's mouth hung open. Reilly was just as dumbfounded. She was trying to figure out when Edward had decided all this. Since they'd talked? Or had he been considering it for days? You never knew with him. He was quite the wily sort. Ray blinked and gave his head a shake, possibly to wake himself from the dream he might have been experiencing. He transferred his gaze to Reilly.

"Did you have anything to do with this?"

"We had a chat, but I never expected it to turn out like this."

Ray looked back to Edward. "Edward…are you *sure* you want to do this?"

He laid a hand gently on Ray's shoulder. "I'm positive. I don't do things halfway." The man could never be accused of that, but *especially* after this.

"Besides the love I've felt this evening is the best Christmas gift I've ever received."

Tara walked up to the group and stood next to Edward. Her expression betrayed that she'd somehow been in on the surprise.

"I have one condition, though." Edward wagged a finger at Ray and adopted a joking tone. "You invite me to next year's Christmas party."

A laugh bubbled up from inside Ray. "Done. You have an open invitation to every Christmas party from here on out." Edward shook Ray's hand.

"Merry Christmas." Ray gave Edward's hand a tug that led to a quick embrace which Reilly joined.

At that moment, Emma excitedly ran up. Emmaline was right behind her.

"Dad guess what?" All vestiges of her adult-esque sophistication were gone. Once again, she was simply an overjoyed twelve-year-old. "Since this is the last night of the Harbor Festival, Topher said the committee decided to vote right away." Her eyes were saucers as she jumped up and down.

"It's unanimous. WE WON!"

"We *won?*" Ray echoed.

"Thanks to Reilly," Emma said.

"It was a team effort." A swell of overjoyed emotion bubbled up in Reilly's heart.

"He said the committee has decided to put in a last-minute, first place prize as well." Emma continued, struggling to catch her breath. "They said they're going to let us keep *The Emma* moored in the harbor for free…*forever!*"

"*Forever?*" Ray's eyes widened.

The crowd of partygoers who'd enjoyed Reilly's mechanical handiwork had now gathered around to hear this good news.

"They said *The Emma* is an historical part of Mistletoe Lake's heritage and therefore should be preserved," Emmaline added with pride.

Then, from the middle of the crowd of onlookers, Topher raised his glass and said, in his most accurate Elvis-like voice yet, "LONG LIVE *THE EMMA!*" The rest of the crowd around the quartette all raised their glasses in a salute.

"MERRY CHRISTMAS!"

As Reilly's gaze moved across all the faces around her—Ray, Emma, Emmaline, Tara—she was overwhelmed with gratitude. This was the most perfect Christmas she could ever dream of having.

"And, Dad, don't worry about Grafton Arts Academy. I've already decided that I'm not going."

"What are you talking about?" Ray gave her a look of pure puzzlement.

Emma pressed on. "Now that you're not selling the boat, we won't have money for the tuition."

"Don't even talk like that. *You're going,*" Ray replied, definitively dismissing her concerns.

"I'm not going, and that's final." Emma did her very best to overrule Ray's parental position, but he only chuckled. Emma had tried to play this one-upmanship game with him before.

"You can't say and that's final to me. *I'm* the parent. I say that to *you.*"

Emma sighed, exasperated. "Dad, please. It's my life. I've made my decision."

A lingering moment passed. Ray then finally said, "So…I suppose we shouldn't open this, then?" From his pocket, he pulled out an envelope. It was addressed to Emma. The return address read *Grafton Arts Academy*. Emma's jaw dropped as soon as she saw it.

"I went to the general store this afternoon to pick up some last-minute things. This was in our mailbox. But, if you're *definitely* not going, then it doesn't matter what the letter says, right?" Ray waved the letter in front of her.

She followed it with her eyes for a moment, like a hypnotist's subject. Then, overcome with curiosity, she snatched it from Ray's hand.

With the letter now in her hands, Emma bit her lower lip, her face dancing with jittery hope marbled with utter dread. She took a breath and slowly tore open the letter. Everyone on the boat waited in suspended animation.

It was dead silent. Emma shakily unfolded the thick stationery paper, neatly folded in thirds. Her eyes moved across the page, taking in the typed words and transmitting them to her brain. When she finally got to the end, the young girl let her head drop, as though she were a masterless marionette, and began to weep in heaving sobs.

As though his playful game had terribly backfired, Ray instantly crouched down and took his daughter by her shoulders, his heart in his throat.

"Em…what does it say?"

Emma could barely speak through her tears. "I…got…" she raised her head and looked at Ray, "…a full scholarship."

Stunned, Ray grabbed the paper and read it himself, his own eyes now filling with emotion. "A full scholarship," he repeated, as though convincing himself he hadn't misheard. Emma was a blubbering mess of joy.

"I secretly applied for a scholarship, but I didn't say anything because I never thought I'd get it and I didn't want to get our hopes up."

Ray was full-on, unabashedly crying now, too. "A FULL SCHOLARSHIP!" he shouted with joy and hugged his little girl. Emmaline, in tears herself, joined in. It was a gorgeous family moment. Ray then pulled Reilly into the group hug, as well. Their audience erupted in another cheer of elation.

Then, Edward noticed Reilly's Christmas gift to Ray sitting in its box nearby.

"Is that a new alternator? We should get it installed and take the boat out for a victory lap. It *is* the Christmas Harbor festival, after all."

Ray nodded. "Now if we only knew someone who could install it." He looked pointedly at Reilly. Before he even said one word, she definitively shook her head and motioned to the beautiful dress she was wearing. There was no way she was going to get under the greasy, archaic engine of the boat.

No. Way.

Chapter 25

As Reilly knelt under the greasy engine of the boat, being *very* careful not to get any grime smudges on her dress or inflict too much damage on the self-pedicure job she'd applied earlier that day, she handed Ray back the wrench and took the rag from him to wipe her hands.

"Okay, Em! Try it now," she yelled up toward the deck. In the boat's cabin, Emma turned the key in the ignition, and the boat's engine thrummed to life. Reilly waited in tense apprehension for the imminent explosion of black soot, but it never came. Instead, the engine purred, ever so eloquently. The gaggle of tipsy onlookers who had watched Reilly display her mechanical skills applauded mightily. It was as though she were a party magician who'd performed a seemingly impossible trick.

Moments later, *The Emma* cruised out on the lake's jet-black water, as though it were a dazzling satellite of love moving through the infinite fathoms of a watery space.

As *The Emma* cruised on what was now its victory lap, Ray stood in the middle of the dance floor on the deck of the boat with Reilly in his arms. The Christmas Eve moon had appeared in the night sky and shone down on them like a celestial spotlight.

"I wanted to tell you…that this boat doesn't just feel like home again because of the way you decorated it," he spoke softly. With all the joyful events of the evening, the two were both spent and at once exhilarated. "From the very moment you set foot on it, your very presence here made me feel at home."

"I feel the same." Reilly could see his soul behind his eyes. "All my life I've been craving the feeling of being at home. And…when I met you, and Emma, I knew that I was." Against the stunning backdrop of Mistletoe Lake, Ray leaned in and kissed her. It was a kiss she could feel at the back of her knees. She tightened her hand around his back and leaned in deeper, as though she could melt into him.

When they finally moved apart, Reilly smiled and gently wiped her lipstick off his mouth. The brand had bragged that it was non-smudge, but they probably hadn't taken into account kisses like that.

"You know, you're not too bad for a City Girl." Ray grinned.

"A Country Boy like you could do a lot worse."

Then something dawned on her.

"Hey…you never told me your middle name."

"Do we know each other well enough for that?" he playfully deflected.

"I think so." Reilly wasn't going to let him off the hook this time.

Ray blushed a little, before saying, "Ignatius."

Reilly exploded into a peal of laughter. *"Ignatius?"*

"It's a family name. On my maternal grandfather's side." This did nothing to quell Reilly's amusement. "You see why I didn't want to tell you?" Ray joined in her laughter.

"I dunno," Reilly replied, "Iggy Mistletoe is a pretty stellar soap-opera name."

"Sounds like some kind of rash."

Now, Reilly was near hysterics. The only thing Ray could do to quieten her was kiss her again. Which he did.

They slowly melted back into each other. Then Emma called from across the deck.

"Hey, you two! We saved one more Christmas surprise for last."

The cold night breeze was tinged with the scent of sugary, homemade goodness as Emma proudly held up a tray of freshly baked confectioneries.

"Christmas nutmeg butter tarts, right out of the oven!"

Hand-in-hand, Reilly and Ray walked over to join the others, as *The Emma* cruised back into the Mistletoe Lake Harbor—its home, forever, shining like a brilliant star in the Christmas Eve sky.

About the Author

Robin Dunne is an actor, writer, and director. His acting career began in 1998 with a supporting role in John Woo-produced *The Big Hit*. Since then, Dunne's other feature film credits include *The Snow Walker, Devil In The Dark, Space Milkshake, Torment*, and *Just Friends*.

His television work includes a leading role in the SyFy Channel's hit series *Sanctuary*, as well as *Dawson's Creek, Dead Like Me, Defiance*, and *October Faction*.

As a writer/director Dunne's credits include *Sanctuary* as well as the films *A.R.C.H.I.E* and *A.R.C.H.I.E 2* (both featuring the voice of Michael J. Fox) as well as *Welcome To Nowhere*, which he also starred in.

Most recently, Dunne has directed the movie of the week *Christmas on Mistletoe Lake* which will premiere on Lifetime. He wrote the screenplay, as well as the novel, which will be released in concert with the film.

In addition, production has also just wrapped on *Making Scents of Love* which Dunne both wrote and directed. The film is set for release in 2023.

Acknowledgements

Firstly, I'd like to thank Dawn Carrington at Vinspire Publishing for taking a chance on someone who'd never written a book in his life. Thank you for all your patience in guiding me through this process.

My wife, Farrah, for your unending encouragement despite my constant whining at how challenging this process was.

My daughter, Everly, for being the inspiration for everything I do.

Robert Vaughn for working as hard as I did to get the movie filmed and delivered even though the universe was constantly conspiring against us.

Genelle Williams, Corey Sevier, and all the actors in the film who took what were just words on a page and breathed life into the characters.

All of our crew who worked tirelessly in harsh exterior conditions.

My agent, Jennifer Goldhar at The Characters, for always being supportive of the strange detours I'm forever taking in my career.

My mom and dad for not only instilling in me the confidence of being able to do whatever I set my mind to, but for giving me a love of reading from a young age.

And finally, Blind Bay—one of my very favorite places in the world and the source of inspiration for this story.

Dear Reader

If you enjoyed reading *Christmas on Mistletoe Lake*, I would appreciate it if you would help others enjoy this book, too. Here are some of the ways you can help spread the word:

Lend it. This book is lending enabled so please share it with a friend.

Recommend it. Help other readers find this book by recommending it to friends, readers' groups, book clubs, and discussion forums.

Share it. Let other readers know you've read the book by positing a note to your social media account and/or your Goodreads account.

Review it. Please tell others why you liked this book by reviewing it on your favorite ebook site.

Everything you do to help others learn about my book is greatly appreciated!

Plan Your Next Escape!
What's Your Reading Pleasure?

Whether it's captivating historical romance, intriguing mysteries, young adult romance, illustrated children's books, or uplifting love stories, Vinspire Publishing has the adventure for you!

For a complete listing of books available, visit our website at www.vinspirepublishing.com.

Like us on Facebook at
www.facebook.com/VinspirePublishing

Follow us on Twitter at
www.twitter.com/vinspire2004

Follow us on Instagram at
www.instagram.com/vinspirepublishing

We are your travel guide to your next adventure!

CPSIA information can be obtained
at www.ICGtesting.com
Printed in the USA
BVHW080924151122
651979BV00006B/153